SHOT DOWN?

"How about Saturday?" persisted Ryan. "A simple yes or no; you don't have to make a big deal of it."

"Because it isn't a simple yes or no," Laura said. "And I'd rather not talk about it with half the class listening."

"I want an answer, Laura."

"Then lean forward so I can whisper it: I *don't* want to be known as one of Lover Boy's girls. I don't need that kind of reputation!"

LOVER BOY

Leila Davis

AN AVON ◯ FLARE BOOK

LOVER BOY is an original publication of Avon Books. This work has never before appeared in book form.

AVON BOOKS
A division of
The Hearst Corporation
105 Madison Avenue
New York, New York 10016

Copyright © 1989 by Leila Davis
Published by arrangement with the author
Library of Congress Catalog Card Number: 88-91358
ISBN: 0-380-75722-2
RL: 6.5

First Avon Flare Printing: April 1989

AVON FLARE TRADEMARK REG. U.S. PAT. OFF. AND IN OTHER COUNTRIES, MARCA REGISTRADA, HECHO EN U.S.A.

Printed in the U.S.A.

K–R 10 9 8 7 6 5 4 3 2

To my husband Ray, for all his support,
and to Diana, Dana, Virginia,
Steve, Billy, and Christina

Special thanks to Scott Henby
for his advice and criticism

Chapter 1

"Enemy action closing in at three o'clock," muttered Matt Maddox, nudging Ryan Archer. "Laura the Libber, and does she ever looked steamed! What did you do this time?"

They leaned against the low brick wall surrounding Lockwood High, enjoying the first really warm day since Easter break. Matt's dark hair and eyes provided a striking contrast to Ryan's almost towheaded blondness. Both boys were tall and lean, dressed in faded jeans and cotton shirts. Ryan turned to watch Laura's approach. They'd been "friendly foes" since seventh grade, with Laura slightly ahead in victories.

"I don't remember scoring any points lately. Maybe she bombed the trig test and I threw the curve by acing it. You know how it grinds her that I'm better at math than she is."

Matt grinned. "That isn't what grinds her; it comes easy for you and she has to work her head off to get the assignments done. Kinda nice to see her humble."

"She doesn't look humble right now. She doesn't look exactly mad, either; more like she's had a bad shock." Ryan's light blue eyes narrowed slightly. "Jeez, she couldn't have flunked the test *that* bad."

1

Ryan stood a little straighter, hooking his thumbs in the back pockets of his jeans. The April sun seemed to take on a chill. Laura stopped directly in front of him, glaring up in a way that minimized the foot difference in height between herself and the two boys. She might be an outspoken antagonist, but Ryan had noticed lately how much prettier her dark hair looked styled in curls.

Her blue eyes bored into his. "Mrs. Kingsley is assigning us parts for *Much Ado About Nothing* today. Did you tell her you wanted any special part?"

The way she said it, it sounded more like an accusation than a question. Ryan forced his tense muscles to relax, refusing to let her put him on the defensive.

"Yeah, I asked to be Borachio. It was about the shortest part I could find. She wouldn't let me be the narrator and read the stage directions again."

He took eleventh grade English because it was required for graduation, and reading Shakespeare aloud ranked with having a tooth filled when it came to things he enjoyed. Laura reveled in it, like all members of the Drama Club.

"She's giving you Benedick instead," said Laura flatly.

Ryan grimaced. "That's one of the long parts."

"It gets worse, Lover Boy. She's assigning me Beatrice. She told me when I was leaving the cafeteria."

"So what? I thought you liked having a long part. Anything, as long as they let you talk."

Laura folded her arms across her nicely rounded chest, an expression of exasperation on her face. "If you had read the introduction, which was assigned

2

for today, you'd know that Benedick and Beatrice are the battling lovers.''

Matt guffawed and Ryan grinned, which only added to Laura's irritation. Her chin took on a more defiant angle.

''You mean I'll be *forced* to shoot you down? And in front of the whole class, too.''

''That's only the beginning. About halfway through the play, they have a big scene where they confess their love for each other and they get married in the end.''

Matt howled louder. Ryan sobered, regarding Laura thoughtfully. He didn't relish the prospect reading of a love scene with her any more than she did. He was even less enthusiastic over the ribbing he'd get from his pals. Laura, of all people! That was worse than a love scene with Martie Purbeck, who was pushing two hundred pounds from the wrong direction.

''Laura, I didn't ask for the part and I don't want it. Why get mad at me?'' He had an uneasy feeling there was more to it than she was telling him. Just then, he caught her flowery scent on the breeze. Funny such a feisty little squirt would wear a perfume so feminine.

''You could ask *not* to have it. I'd rather read a love scene with Laughing Boy here than have to read one with you!''

''The feeling is mutual, Miss Nettleton,'' said Ryan stiffly. Who did she think she was?

''Good! Please talk to Mrs. Kingsley before class. You know she won't change her mind once she announces it.''

Matt, still grinning, interrupted. ''I think we should circle this date on the calendar and declare it a national holiday. You two actually agreed on something.''

"If Mrs. Kingsley is casting according to type, you're sure to be Dogberry." Laura gave him a scathing glance, which didn't faze him. "Dogberry has that famous line, 'Remember, that I am an ass.' "

Matt reddened. Ryan looked at him out of the corner of his eye. Laura *had* to be worked up to take shots at poor Matt. She usually saved her heavy artillery for him.

"You should know better than to give her an opening," he said under his breath to Matt, then turned back to Laura. "It sounds like you've read the whole thing."

"I have. Mrs. Kingsley also let me take home the videotape of it last night."

"Did she say it's definite I have to be Benedick?"

"No. She said she thought you might do well in the part. I suggested three others but she doesn't think they'd read it as well. Much as it pained me, I had to agree."

The warning bell signaled the end of lunch period. Moving toward the building, Ryan tried to figure out the best way to approach Mrs. Kingsley. Even if some other girl were Beatrice, he still didn't want to read any more of the archaic Shakespearean language than necessary.

"I'll try to get to class early," he told Laura. "But I think you'd have a better chance of winning an argument with her. You're Michigan's champion debater, not me."

"I placed fifth in State, not first, and I need better grounds for an argument than the fact that we don't get along. If you were an idiot, I could say you couldn't handle the part. Unfortunately, you *can* handle it. Some people might even say the play was written with us in mind."

4

The distress in her voice set off an alarm in Ryan's brain. What was she holding back? He opened the door, motioning Laura ahead of him.

"If you're all that upset about it, why don't you ask her to get somebody else for Beatrice?"

The look Laura gave him would stop a torpedo. "Unfortunately, I made a big deal of telling her I wanted the part and borrowing the tape. It's in your hands, Lover Boy, and unless you want to give new meaning to that name, you'd better convince her!"

Laura disappeared down the hall, still bristling with hostility. Ryan glared after her. Under different circumstances, he might appreciate the feminine swing of her hips in those tapered blue pants. Today he felt more like giving her a solid kick on her backside.

He and Matt made their way to the second floor to collect their books for physics. Neither said a word until they stopped in front of their battered gray lockers, but Ryan caught Matt giving him a worried look.

"Think you can talk Kingsley out of it?" asked Matt.

"I hope so." Ryan broke into a mischievous grin. "On the other hand, I can't think of anything that would annoy Laura more than hearing me say 'I love you' in front of the whole class. She'd cringe like she does everytime somebody drags their fingernails across the board."

Matt grinned back at him. "It *would* be funny. I can just see her sitting there with that determined expression she gets on her face whenever she's being 'self-controlled.' I'm sorry I didn't read it now."

"Aw, she's probably going off the deep end about nothing. Maybe she thinks I'll ruin the play by not being serious enough about it."

5

While supposedly watching a movie in physics class, Ryan's mind wandered to Laura. Now that he'd gotten over his irritation, he could savor their latest exchange. Funny, over the years he'd always enjoyed the classes with her more than any others. Days when they had a verbal duel, he'd go home on an emotional high, regardless of who won.

Not that the duels ever bothered Laura much. *Nothing* bothered Laura much! Even when she asked dumb questions in trig and everybody jeered at her, she carried it off with poise. Ryan knew he'd never have the nerve to ask a question again if kids laughed at him like that.

The film momentarily caught Ryan's attention when the actor explained how NASA scientists calculated the thrust necessary to launch a missile. As an avid collector and builder of model rockets, Ryan often had to make the same kind of calculations. When the talk focused on funding, he tuned the film out.

His pals didn't think much of Laura. She could take on the whole gang at one time and whip them with one well-worded sentence. Unfortunately, they took defeat harder than Ryan did. They might like her better if they scored a victory once in a while. They never missed a chance to cut down The Libber, starting with the name they'd tagged on her. She'd accepted the tag as a compliment.

Something about her had attracted him that first day he saw her in their junior high social studies class. Maybe it was her self-confidence. Her sharp wit had fascinated him from the beginning, even when he was her target. She was the only person he knew who never worried about giving oral reports in front of the class. Or the whole school, like she sometimes did as Junior Class President.

Why couldn't she be more like Therese, the reigning class beauty? That girl knew how to make a guy feel like a million bucks in more ways than one. Therese had taught Ryan the finer points of kissing, then dubbed him "Lover Boy." She'd made it plain she was willing to teach him a lot more.

Ryan's thoughts drifted back to Laura. Why was she making such a fuss about reading some ancient play? Ordinarily she didn't care what anybody said about them or their battles. Unless she came off second best all the way through this play. Ryan grinned. Being on the losing end would get her steamed up for sure. He hoped that was the reason.

Physics over, Ryan and Matt quickly worked their way through the crowded hall to their English class at the opposite end of the second floor. Mrs. Kingsley sat at her cluttered desk, making notes about the last class. Ryan nervously waited for her to glance up.

"I don't believe it—you're actually early today." Her smile softened her features, making her look less intimidating. "Are you that eager to get started or do you want an excuse from class again to go work on some science project?"

"I heard you were assigning parts for us to read today and just wanted to remind you that I'd like to be Borachio. Or Conrade," said Ryan anxiously.

Her eyebrows rose fractionally. "The short parts again, hmmm? Sorry, I let you have short parts in *Macbeth* and *Julius Caesar*. It's your turn for a long one."

"Which long one?" asked Ryan, his throat going dry.

"Benedick. Laura will read Beatrice. The way you two are always dueling, I thought you might enjoy the chance to do it officially."

7

"I wouldn't mind being Benedick," said Matt hastily.

Mrs. Kingsley leaned back to study him. Her chair creaked as she shifted her weight. "You wouldn't, huh? Yesterday you begged to be the villainous Prince John."

"Ryan could be Prince John."

"Greater love hath no man than that he read Shakespeare for his friend," paraphrased Mrs. Kingsley. "Nice try, but it's still Ryan's turn for a long part."

"I owe you one," mumbled Ryan as they crossed to their seats. By some fluke, he sat directly behind Laura, with Matt across the aisle. "She won't believe I tried to get out of this. Maybe I should have asked to be one of the other long parts."

Matt nodded toward the door. "Here she comes."

"You have to do it," said Laura, sliding her books onto the desk. She sighed audibly. "Well, we'll just have to muddle through the best we can."

"I don't know what you're griping about," said Ryan. "Benedick's part is longer than Beatrice's. Or is that what's making you sore?"

"Ryan, when you were looking at all those lines Benedick has, if you'd *read* some of them instead of just *counting* them, you'd know why I'm not too thrilled about it." She turned her back on him, then abruptly turned around again. "When you *do* read it, you're going to be a lot unhappier than I am. I'm used to being heckled."

"Heckled? It's a moldy old play. How bad can it be?"

"Stop the talking back there," said Mrs. Kingsley. "I want to get class started."

A word from the teacher always silenced Laura. Today, it added to Ryan's stress. The stuffy room suddenly seemed suffocating. He asked permission and was allowed to open a window.

After roll, Mrs. Kingsley assigned parts for the play. "I'd like you to put a little feeling into your roles, which means it would be helpful for you at least to skim the play before class, if you can't bring yourselves to read it twice. We should be finished reading Thursday. We'll go over the study guide Friday, see the videotape next week, have our test, and wind up the Shakespeare unit."

Assorted cheers interrupted her. She waited patiently for the class to settle down again.

"Your enthusiasm for Shakespeare is positively underwhelming. The sooner we get at this, the sooner we'll finish. Angela, read the introduction."

Once they started reading, Ryan rather enjoyed the sharp exchanges between Beatrice and Benedick and needed no urging to put "feeling" into it. Laura really was coming off second best as Beatrice. The class was soon caught up in this play, which did sound a little as if it had been written about Laura and Ryan. For the first time, the kids could believe Mrs. Kingsley's comment that Shakespeare wrote about universal themes and characters.

"You were meant to be Beatrice," said Ryan, tapping Laura's shoulder at the end of the period. "Benedick was right on when he called her Lady Disdain. You do 'speak poniards and stab with every word.' What I don't understand is how Shakespeare knew what you'd be like four hundred years before you were born."

Laura turned around, refusing to be ruffled by his teasing. "Before you get carried away with all your gloating, you'd better read the rest of the play. I have a hunch you'll find it a lot harder to put feeling into your role when we get to Act IV, Scene I, even with your image as a hot lover. The last three pages; look it up.''

Ryan and Matt exchanged glances. A queasy sensation gripped Ryan, as if he'd just put his foot in it. Maybe he should take his English book home tonight. Better to be prepared than to get an unpleasant shock in front of the whole class. That was the second time today Laura had mentioned his Lover Boy image. She had to have a reason.

"It didn't go too bad today," said Matt on the way out to the parking lot beyond the waiting buses.

"I think I'll survive it. When we get to the proposal scene, Benedick probably demands what would have been like a million bucks back in those days to marry her. Can't you see Laura squirming over that? Funny!''

"Yeah. Well, it'll be—''

"Hi, Lover Boy,'' interrupted Therese Deauville. "How about giving me a ride home?''

Ryan smiled, then whistled at the way Therese's scooped neck top and tight jeans displayed her figure. The sun glinted on her long chestnut hair, picking up the coppery highlights. She smiled at him flirtatiously, slipping an arm around his waist and rubbing against his thigh.

"No problem.'' Ryan stole a quick kiss as his arm encircled her. There was nothing subtle about her perfume. He wished they had a few classes together so he could see her more often. She was so popular that he sometimes felt like he had to take a number to see her.

"Catch you later,'' said Matt, splitting off to his car.

Ryan unlocked the passenger door of his red vintage Volkswagen Bug and held it for Therese. Seated beside her a moment later, he rolled down the window, then joined the cars jockeying to get out of the parking lot. Therese switched on the radio in time for them to hear that the temperature was seventy-eight with an overnight low of forty-five expected.

"So when are you getting a better car?" asked Therese. "I don't know why you ever bought something this small anyway, as tall as you are."

Ryan's car had been a sore point between them ever since he'd bought it. He took pride in restoring the Beetle, keeping it in top condition. Therese liked big, fast cars and the guys who had them. She didn't see much status in a Bug bordering on the antique, no matter how well kept.

"You knew what kind of a car I have when you asked for a ride," he said sharply. "If it isn't good enough for you, why didn't you ask somebody else?"

Therese's manner promptly changed. She snuggled as close to him as she could with the stick shift in the way. Ryan felt his pulse quicken when she placed her hand on his thigh, slowly massaging it.

"Don't be mad, Lover Boy. You know there's nobody I'd rather kiss goodbye than you. You do it so *well*."

Her words brought that peculiar mixture of embarrassment and pride he'd felt ever since she'd nicknamed him Lover Boy last fall. The guys kidded him about it, but it did give him a special status in their group. Ryan would die if they ever found out how undeserved the name really was.

"I'm not mad; just don't hassle me about my car."

"I promise I'll apologize beautifully when we get to my house," she said with a seductive giggle.

11

Ryan shook his head. "I have to be at work by three. Jobs are too hard to find for me to lose this one."

"You mean you'd rather go work in a smelly gas station than spend a few minutes with me?" Maybe she was only teasing but it sounded to Ryan more like she was really ticked off. She moved back in her seat.

He glanced at her quickly. "It's not what I'd *rather* do; it's what I have to do. My car insurance is coming up."

He slowed to turn the corner to Therese's house, gliding the short distance to her driveway. Much as he'd like to go in, the clock on the dashboard warned him he had just enough time to make it to work.

Therese pulled him toward her, pressing her mouth firmly against his. Ryan's arms tightened around her. At moments like this, he wished he did have a bigger car. Once again he had the heady sensation of playing with fire. So what always compelled him to stop before he got burned?

"Are you sure you can't come in for a few minutes?" she whispered. "No one's home."

"I get off work at six. What if I come by later?"

"Later's no good. Mom and Joe will be home then."

Ryan knew without asking that Therese's stepfather didn't allow any "visiting behind closed doors" when he was home. "Are you busy Friday night?"

"Yes, I am. I wish you'd asked sooner."

"How about Saturday?" He didn't really expect her to accept. Sometimes he wondered why he kept asking. Still . . .

"I . . . uh . . . have to go to my cousin's wedding."

Something about her tone when she said it and the

12

way she studied her nails told Ryan she was lying. Come to think of it, she'd been seeing a lot of Jeff Yarbrough lately, ever since he got that Fiero. Cars counted more than guys with Therese.

"Some other time," said Ryan, hoping he sounded nonchalant. "Well, I have to get to work."

His job, a necessity with a car to maintain and insure, kept Ryan off the baseball team this spring. Having sacrificed baseball, he wasn't about to risk losing his job for a couple of hours with any girl, not even Therese.

Ryan parked behind the station on the stroke of three. Mr. Dennison's six o'clock closing hour was for his convenience, not that of his customers. A widower, he liked spending his evenings in pursuit of the "big win" in bingo. Ryan would have preferred longer hours for the money but appreciated having his evenings and Sundays free.

"How many jackpots did you win last night?" Ryan asked, hoping to divert attention from the time. He took his dark blue overalls from the peg and slipped them on.

"Twenty-five dollars, hardly enough to make it worth carrying home," groused the older man. He sat hunched in a cracked vinyl chair. "Cost me more than that to play."

"Maybe you should get acquainted with that woman over in Winslow who won the lottery. I heard she's a widow."

"Don't think I haven't thought of it, son. When you get time, clean out the restrooms. Some woman complained today about mud all over the floor."

Mr. Dennison blew his nose on one of the big bandanna handkerchiefs he carried, then stuffed it back in the pocket of his greasy overalls. The handkerchief had its share of grease, too. Ryan often wondered why his boss didn't use a Kleenex, then throw it away. It wasn't as if the stuff cost a fortune.

Dennison's wasn't a big chain gas station. Over the years, the premises had slowly deteriorated but the service was always good. Good enough to guarantee a steady stream of loyal customers. It was also the only station still operating in this quiet part of town.

Today they were busy, with more customers than usual wanting personal service. While Ryan washed windows or checked oil, he thought about Therese and Laura. Total opposites. Therese loved sexy clothes, big cars, and being popular with the guys. Laura didn't date much and dressed nicely but didn't follow the fads. He remembered seeing her at the Sweetheart Formal but couldn't remember who she was with. Not one of the guys in his crowd.

Ryan checked his own oil and gassed up before going home, scrupulously putting his money in the till. One of the guys at school had actually been dumb enough to ask if Ryan got his gas free now. That would be the day!

Ryan parked his Bug in the garage beside his father's Oldsmobile shortly after six, then entered the raised ranch-style house through the laundry room. Only salespeople or his grandparents ever used the front door.

The tantalizing aroma of pork chops greeted him. Dad got off work at four-thirty, like the majority of workers in Lockwood, and expected dinner to be on the table by five. Family tradition didn't change when Ryan got a job.

"Your supper's in the oven," called Mom from the family room when she heard him come in. "Your favorite, stuffed pork chops and mashed potatoes. There's some banana cream pie, too, if your sister didn't eat it all.''

"I left a piece for him," protested Cheryl.

"Matt called; he wants you to call back," continued Mom.

"I think I'll shower first and get cleaned up. It might get rid of this gas smell," said Ryan. He paused at the family room door, glancing at his mother French braiding Cheryl's light brown hair. "Any mail?"

"Brochures from three more colleges. I left them on the table by your place.''

"Unless they're offering money, forget it." His score of 177 points on the PSAT had interested several colleges, though he'd missed the 192 points necessary to qualify for a National Merit Scholarship.

Forty-five minutes later, Ryan carried the phone into his bedroom and dialed Matt's number. "What's up?"

"Have you got your English book at home?"

"Yeah, I thought I'd skim over it if I had time when I finish our physics assignment."

"Look on page 241, left column, halfway down. I think it's the part Laura meant."

Ryan put down the phone to get the book he'd left on the kitchen counter. "Okay, I'm back. What page was it?"

"Bottom half of 241. Those short lines between Beatrice and Benedick."

Ryan skimmed the lines quickly then groaned when he read Benedick's declaration of love. It wasn't a joke after all. Yes, it was, on Ryan. He could hear the class howl when he read that aloud. Why hadn't he listened to Laura?

"I take it you found the part," said Matt. "Thought I'd better warn you. If it's any comfort, I don't think Laura's going to enjoy it either."

Ryan hung up and sat there, staring at the book. He read the remainder of the scene, his stomach knotting up more with each line. The relationship between the lovers in their quarreling phase paralleled too closely his relationship with Laura. He knew the kids would read a double meaning into every word. Ryan dropped his head in his hands.

"Oh Lord, please don't let me turn red when they laugh."

Chapter 2

Ryan paced back and forth in his room, an exercise limited to the small area of carpet between his extra-long bed and the desk, bookshelves, and dresser opposite. He stumbled once over one of his running shoes. A swift kick sent it under the bed. At this precise moment, he wished he could crawl inside one of the many model rockets displayed around the room and blast off into outer space.

After the way Mrs. Kingsley refused to let Matt take his role, he knew she wouldn't let him off the hook now. She'd say he was making "much ado about nothing." Damn William Shakespeare!

Ryan ran a nervous hand through his flaxen hair. *If I pretend I'm sick for three days, Mom will haul me in to the doctor. And if I cut English for three days, I'll be suspended, not to mention the guys saying I was chicken.*

He sat on the edge of his bed, elbows resting on his spread knees, hands tightly folded. He didn't want to be a laughingstock. Okay, play it for laughs. They'd be laughing with him, not at him. Really go overboard with the "I love you" lines.

I hope it works. I should have known Laura wouldn't

ask me to get out of it if it weren't serious. If I clown it up, Laura might do the same. Yeah—she's got a sense of humor. We have to do something to keep everybody from dying of boredom.

The next day, Ryan's tension steadily mounted until English. He tried forcing himself to relax so that his nerves wouldn't show through in his voice. By now he'd abandoned the idea of being a clown. The kids would never let him live it down if the joke fell flat. Better to read it straight. And Laura sat there in front of him, talking to Cindy about forensics class as calmly as if they only had to recite the alphabet.

"Since this is the last class of the day, let's put the desks in a circle," said Mrs. Kingsley. "Wealthy patrons used to sit on the stage of the Globe Theatre during the original performances of Shakespeare."

Chairs scraped and voices babbled while the desks were dragged into a new formation. Ryan and Laura now found themselves side by side. Matt sat on her left.

"I hope you read this," whispered Laura, leaning slightly toward Ryan.

"I did. Maybe somebody will nuke the school and we won't have to read it."

Laura grinned. "You're such an optimist! I'd settle for a fire drill."

"A fire drill wouldn't destroy the school and the books. We'd just have to read it later."

The class read through the conspiracy to slander innocent Hero, the arrest of the villains, and Claudio's rejection of Hero at their wedding. Ryan privately thought Hero was a dumb name for the heroine. If you didn't know the story, you'd think a couple of guys were getting married.

Neither Ryan nor Laura, as supporting characters,

18

though important ones, had many lines up to then. As they approached their declaration of love scene, following Hero's faked death, both of them tensed up. Perspiration trickled down Ryan's chest and ribs. Out of the corner of his eye, he watched Laura do some deep breathing, trying to relax. He took a deep breath of his own before reading the fatal line.

" 'I do love nothing in the world so well as you. Is not that strange?' " Ryan felt his ears grow warm at the sound of stifled snickers.

" 'As strange as the thing I know not,' " replied Laura. " 'It were as possible for me to say I loved nothing so well as you: but believe me not; and yet I lie not; I confess nothing, nor I deny nothing—I am sorry for my cousin.' "

Ryan noticed that the self-possessed Laura turned pink, which made it a little easier to read his next line. " 'By my sword, Beatrice, thou lovest me.' " For one crazy second, he wished it were true.

Am I going nuts? Why would I want Laura to love me? That would be the moment he noticed what soft pink lips she had. His mind was still absorbed with Laura's lips when she kicked his ankle and brought him back to the script.

The ensuing lines came easier as they got into Beatrice's demand that Benedick kill Claudio for rejecting Hero. Ryan felt more comfortable arguing with Laura. Maybe he could get a laugh yet, defuse all this "romance."

When he reached his last line, he put action to words when he said, " 'I will kiss your hand.' " He accomplished it so smoothly that it was over before Laura had a chance to object.

"Way to go, Lover Boy!" shouted someone from the other side of the room.

Ryan grinned sheepishly and winked at Laura. The surprised expression on her face quickly gave way to anger and for a moment, he thought she'd slap him. She simply averted her face, refusing to look at him again.

"That's the end of the scene, so we'll stop there for today," said Mrs. Kingsley. "Put your desks back in order. Quickly, before the bell rings. And Ryan, try to keep your amorous impulses under control tomorrow."

"Yes, ma'am."

Under cover of moving desks, Ryan tried to assess Laura's feelings. Why hadn't she made some caustic remark? He'd even been prepared to duck in case she took a swing at him. Didn't she know it was a joke? She shoved her desk into place and sat rigidly facing the front of the room, ignoring the jibes of kids around her.

As soon as the bell rang, Laura was out of her seat and halfway to the door before Ryan could get up.

"She is one mad lady," mumbled Matt.

"Yeah. I guess I'd better apologize. I didn't expect her to take it like that."

He found her at her locker, still taut with anger. Ryan stood behind her, waiting for the hall to clear so they could talk privately. Laura slammed her locker shut and headed for the stairs, ignoring Ryan's existence.

"Laura, I'm sorry," he said, catching up with her. "I only meant it as a joke."

She kept walking, dodging around the kids in front of her. "Very funny. Ha, ha. Show the world what a great lover you are."

"What are you so upset about? We've been battling for years and it's never bothered you before."

She swung around to face him, her eyes blazing. "You've never tried a cheap shot before! Being shot down is one thing but you deliberately embarrassed me."

"Cheap shot! I wasn't taking a cheap shot. Don't you think you're overreacting a little? All I did was kiss your hand; it wasn't any big passionate love scene."

"You're right," she said, lowering her eyes. She swallowed hard. "I am overreacting. It wasn't that important."

She abruptly turned and ran out the door, jumping aboard her bus before he could catch her. Ryan stared at the bus for a moment, then returned to his locker. He found Matt waiting for him.

"She's still mad?"

Ryan shrugged, impatiently jamming his books onto the shelf. "She said it was a cheap shot." He paused, leaning one hand against the locker as he turned to look at Matt. "She isn't just mad. I hurt her feelings. I thought she'd slap me or say something really cutting but I sure never expected her to be *hurt*."

"Yeah, it is strange she'd take it that way. She's so self-confident and assertive that you never think of her having hurt feelings."

The incident continued to prey on Ryan's mind all the time he was at work. Laura's taut figure haunted him.

Why did I ever do such a stupid thing? It wasn't that funny. I was so determined not to let on how embarrassed I was that I embarrassed Laura. I guess it really was a cheap shot. She looked almost ready to cry. Laura never cries.

His crazy brain had to pick that moment to wonder

if her lips were as warm as her hand. Then it had to start conjuring up images of Laura in his arms, and Ryan knew it was time for drastic action, such as cleaning the restrooms again. Nothing like ammonia to cure romantic fantasies.

Driving home, Ryan passed Francine's Flower Shoppe and made an abrupt turn into the driveway, which inspired a few choice words from the driver behind him. Squealing brakes and honking horns added a few more decibels.

The shop was warm and humid and smelled of moist earth. A philodendron, trained to grow over the doorway, caught at his hair as he passed under it. Ryan looked around for signs of something alive that wasn't rooted in potting soil.

"May I help you?" asked the clerk, a tall woman with half framed glasses and a name tag that said "Francine."

"Yeah. I . . . uh . . . want some flowers for a girl, but I'm not sure what she likes." *Why did I ever come in here? I have less than five bucks in my pocket.*

"A corsage for a dance?" inquired Francine, peering intently at him.

"No, it's . . . uh . . . more of an apology."

"Sweetheart roses are eighteen dollars a dozen or we have a special on daisies this week for ten dollars."

Ryan gulped, sorrier than ever that he'd stopped. He glanced around the shop, trying to think of a way to make a graceful exit. The clerk thawed a little.

"Some girls think a single rose is very romantic. Our smaller ones sell for one dollar."

"She might like that," conceded Ryan.

"What color would you like?"

He studied the assortment behind the big glass

22

doors of the cooler. The coral ones were pretty. He could write something on the card about being the thorn in her side. Thorns. Laura would appreciate that. His gaze traveled around the shop, studying the plants displayed on the open shelves until he found a small cactus with two plastic eyes on the top.

"How much is that cactus?"

"Cactus? Are you sure this is an apology?"

Ryan grinned. "If she's still mad, she'd get more satisfaction out of throwing a cactus at me than a rose."

Francine's mouth formed into a grim line of disapproval. Ryan decided she must not have much of a sense of humor. She put some green florist's paper into a box and placed the cactus on top of it. He filled out a card for Laura while Francine rang up the sale.

Ryan slowly drove down Mulberry, looking for the Nettletons' white Cape Cod house. Low growing yews bordered the front of it, and a tall oak stood just off the garage. Assorted tulips and daffodils lined the walk, coaxed into bloom by the warmer than usual weather of the past week.

He parked in the driveway, then sat staring at the house for a moment. What seemed like a good idea in the flower shop didn't seem quite so funny when he actually rang the doorbell. What if Laura wasn't home? But why shouldn't she be; it was only six-thirty-five.

Why do I keep doing these dumb things? Maybe I should have gotten the rose.

A slender man with a receding hairline and piercing blue eyes opened the door. He stood there, silently waiting for Ryan to say something. It would have to be her father who came to the door. Ryan might be half a foot taller but he suddenly felt like he was about nine years old. The smell of roast beef reminded his stomach that it hadn't been fed.

"Is Laura home?" Ryan's throat felt dry again.

"She's in the kitchen doing dishes." Mr. Nettleton stood aside, nodding toward the open archway opposite. "Laura, you've got a visitor."

"Tell whoever it is to come in," she called. "I'm right in the middle of washing the dutch oven."

Ryan crossed the living room in three strides, barely conscious of the TV news report he'd interrupted. He stopped just inside the archway, first making sure he was out of Mr. Nettleton's line of vision.

Laura hummed softly while she scrubbed a black cast-iron kettle. She looked quite pretty in pink shorts and a pink-and-white-striped shirt. Now he was noticing her legs and what slender ankles she had. Why had he started looking at Laura as a girl rather than a fencing partner? Ryan waited silently for her to finish with her work.

"Be with you in a minute," she said, rinsing the kettle. When she turned and saw Ryan, her eyes widened with surprise. "Oh. I thought it was Sue."

"Hope you don't mind," said Ryan feebly.

"No. Sit down."

She waved toward the round maple table at the right end of the room. Ryan pulled back one of the captain's chairs and lowered himself onto a brown-and-rust-patchwork-patterned cushion. He set the box on the quilted placemat in front of him. Fragrant narcissi brightened the table.

Laura drained and rinsed the sink, then joined him at the table, a baffled expression on her face. "Um . . . would you like a Coke?"

"No, thanks. I just got off work and have to get

home for supper." He awkwardly handed her the white florist's box. "I'm sorry about what happened today."

"Forget it. You don't have to give me presents."

The box sat there between them, unopened. Ryan felt his ears getting warm again and wished he'd gone straight home. Laura's eyes softened and she reached for the box.

"I didn't mean to sound like a jerk. It was nice of you to bring me something."

"That's okay. I told the woman at the store you might throw it at me."

She had to break the cellophane tape to get the box open. After parting the green paper, two glassy eyes stared up at her. Laura smiled, then lifted out the cactus in its little red clay pot. She shook it gently to make the eyes wiggle, then peeked into the box for a card.

" 'To Laura from the number-one thorn in your life,' " she read. "Does this mean I can expect the thorns to multiply?"

"No. I don't want to lose my favorite enemy. My life would be pretty dull if I didn't have you around to argue with, Lady Disdain."

"You'd better be careful about what you borrow from that play. Remember what happened to Benedick when he started being nice to Beatrice."

"That's because everybody plotted to make them think each was secretly in love with the other. That's not the case with us."

Laura set the plant on the table, keeping her eyes on it. Her face turned almost as pink as her shirt. Ryan caught his breath. Laura couldn't possibly like him. . . .

"I think they were in love with each other all

along but neither one wanted to admit it for fear of rejection," she said, her voice sounding a little strained.

"Aw, come on. The way they were cutting each other down at the start of that play? What I don't believe is the sudden change."

"It wasn't sudden," said Laura, shaking her head. "Go back and reread it. Beatrice's very first line asks if Benedick survived the war. She wouldn't have done that if she weren't worried about him."

"Okay, maybe she did have a thing for him. He didn't think much of her."

Laura looked him straight in the eyes, ready to do battle. Ryan relaxed. Arguments he could handle.

"Oh, no? When Claudio asked his opinion of Hero, Benedick said Beatrice was more beautiful. All through the play are little clues that they're in love. It really comes through on the videotape. The way they interacted was so neat. And I *loved* the actor who played Benedick."

"I guess anything is possible in Shakespeare. He turned Romeo and Juliet into lovers." Ryan stood, relieved that Laura had accepted the apology. "I'd better get home or Mom will be wondering what happened to me."

Laura rose also. "Thank you for the plant. I think I'll call him Benedick."

"You talk to your plants?" He might have expected that of Laura.

"Mm-hmm, and if you find your ears burning, you'll know I'm talking about you!"

"Watch what you say, Lady Disdain. I trained him to shoot those thorns."

"A booby-trapped cactus, huh? In that case, I'll win him over to my side before I fill him in on the real you. Did you meet my father?"

26

"He let me in but I didn't tell him who I was."

"Daddy isn't much for spontaneous conversation. Mom's at her aerobics class or she'd have talked your ear off."

Laura led the way back to the living room and introduced Ryan to her father, now reading the paper more than watching the news. Mr. Nettleton lowered his paper to look Ryan over curiously.

"So you're the Archer boy. The way Laura's talked about you all these years, I expected a combination of Dracula, Frankenstein, and the Three Stooges."

Laura's face flamed red. Ryan laughed nervously.

"My dad always says you shouldn't believe anything you hear and only half of what you see."

"He has a point. It was nice meeting you. Hope we'll see you more often."

Laura hustled Ryan out of the house, still embarrassed over her father's disclosure.

"Do you really talk about me?" he asked, unexpectedly flattered.

"Sometimes I mention it when we've had a go-round at school." She wouldn't look at him when she said it.

"You don't have to be embarrassed about it. I talk about you at home sometimes, too."

"Yeah? Well, thanks for Benedick. And if you ever do anything like that in class again, I'll come after you with a chainsaw, not a little cactus."

Ryan laughed. "That sounds more like the girl I love to pick on. I'll have to read that play thoroughly and see what I can do tomorrow to liven it up."

"You liven it up any more and you'll be dead!"

"Such violent words from such a little squirt," said Ryan, pretending to lean his elbow on top of her

27

head. "You're so close to the ground, I'll have to be careful where I step. You might bite my ankles."

"Goliath didn't have much respect for David either, and look what happened to him."

"You mean you're an expert with a slingshot? There's no end to your talents."

"Remember that." Laura looked past him to his shining Beetle. "That's the neatest car! Is it yours?"

Ryan glowed with pride. "Yeah, I restored it. Took me all winter. The left front fender is new and I had to put a new floor under the driver's side. Mechanically, it wasn't in too bad shape for its age. It just turned over 100,000 on the odometer."

"Beautiful job. This paint shines like a mirror. I love these little Bugs. Someday when I'm filthy rich, that's the kind of car I want." Laura lovingly stroked the smooth surface of the hood.

"Yeah? I thought girls liked big, sleek cars."

Laura shook her head. "No way. In most standard-size cars, the top of the steering wheel is right at my eye level. And I have to move the seat way forward to reach the pedals. A Bug is just my size."

"I take a lot of kidding because it *isn't* my size. I have to move the seat all the way back." He patted the car affectionately. "I wouldn't trade it, though, for anything less than a Porsche."

"I just happen to have a couple cluttering up the garage. Want to swap?" asked Laura, looking up with laughing eyes.

"Ryan's Revenge is worth more than two measly Porsches. I'd have to get at least six to one."

"I'll work on it."

"Speaking of work, if I don't get home, Mom'll be calling Mr. Dennison to find out what happened to me."

28

He slid under the steering wheel and turned on the ignition. Laura watched him from the lawn, arms folded across her chest, a smile on her lips.

"Thanks for the cactus. It's much more symbolic than ordinary roses."

Ryan pondered that on the way home. The cactus *was* symbolic of their relationship, prickly but enduring. So Laura talked about him at home. Funny how that made him feel good. And she liked his car. He was right to apologize; Laura was too good an adversary to lose.

Tonight was Dad's bowling night and Mom had gone to a neighbor's. Cheryl sat in the family room, munching popcorn and watching MTV. Ryan, trying to study in his room, yelled at her to turn the volume down. She turned it up. He stormed into the family room, ready to rip the plug out of the wall. Cheryl ran to the TV, turned down the set, then stuck her tongue out at him.

Ryan glared, his fists clenched. "You turn that thing up again and I'll shove your head through the screen."

"You turn it up louder than that when you want to watch it. Stuff your ears with cotton."

After a few more threats and counterthreats, Ryan went back to his room and slammed the door. He stretched out on the bed with his English book to look for parts he'd have with Laura. Now he felt excited about exchanging barbs with her. Their next encounter was the garden scene after Benedick challenged Claudio.

Laura's words came to mind, saying that Beatrice and Benedick had been in love all along. Ryan paid more attention to their lines, in which each both denied and admitted love.

" 'Thou and I are too wise to woo peaceably.' "
Ryan read the line three times.

Did that describe Laura and him? Could Laura possibly like him? He put the book down to pursue that line of thought for a few minutes. What would it be like to actually hold Laura? . . .

At about eight-thirty, Matt dropped in with Jason Pringle, Peter McCabe, and Craig Swenson, the guys Ryan liked to hang out with. Ryan invited them to his room—away from the nuisance of Cheryl, who currently had a crush on Peter—and passed out Cokes.

"Hear you scored a few points on the Libber today," said Peter, the acknowledged hunk of the group. Cheryl wasn't the only girl affected by his perfect tan, brown eyes, and honey-colored hair. He leaned against the wall, one foot lazily crossed over the other.

"It doesn't count when she doesn't fight back," said Ryan tightly.

"I'll bet she never washes her hand again," kidded Craig. "It has to be a thrill when some guy kisses *her*."

Ryan regarded the husky redhead with annoyance. Putting down Laura was his prerogative, nobody else's. "Laura's not so bad."

"So what are you planning for tomorrow?" asked Peter. "We're reading that play in third period and the last scene has Benedick kiss Beatrice on the mouth."

"Aw, jeez," interrupted Jason, a beanpole just starting a growth spurt and the only one under six feet. "Have a heart! Who'd want to kiss the Libber on the mouth? Granted, it would be the thrill of her life, but think of the psychological damage to the guy."

"Look guys, could we just cool it with Laura?" said Ryan. "I'm getting bored with all this talk about Laura, Laura, Laura."

He hoped that sounded convincing. They'd laugh themselves sick if they knew what had been going through his mind a few minutes ago.

Peter winked. "Think what a favor you'd be doing her."

"If you're that interested in doing her a favor, *you* kiss her," said Matt. "Don't dump it on Ryan."

"Can't, I'm not in her class. So what do you say, Ryan? I'll bet five bucks you haven't got the guts to kiss her when you read that line."

"I told you, I don't want to kiss her. I've got an image to think of," he said, trying to make light of it. "Kissing Laura won't do anything for me."

"You're not afraid of her, are you?" jibed Peter.

"Be serious! It's like Matt said, you want to do her a favor, you kiss her. I've got my standards."

"I'll add three bucks to that pot," said Craig.

Jason checked the contents of his wallet and nodded. "I'm in for a couple. That's ten, Ryan buddy. Think you could force yourself to kiss the Libber for ten bucks?"

"I wouldn't kiss her for a hundred!"

"I wouldn't either, but the most we can come up with is ten," said Peter. "Let's see it, guys."

"Don't bother; I won't do it!" Ryan snapped.

"Won't cost you a cent, good buddy," soothed Peter. "Matt can hold the dough. You kiss her on the mouth, it's yours. Just to prove you've got the guts."

Peter, Jason, and Craig solemnly handed the money to Matt. He reluctantly accepted it. Ryan couldn't believe his eyes. As chronically short of money as they always were, they had to be positive he'd chicken out. When they started out, they were putting down Laura; now they were carving up him. He felt as if he'd been caught in quicksand.

"What's with you guys?" demanded Ryan. "You aren't even in the class to see it."

"It'd be worth ten bucks just to show that mouthy female there are still a few men left in the world. You're the only one with the opportunity. You're doing it for all the male chauvinists she's dumped on," said Peter.

The boys left shortly afterward. Ryan lay on his bed, in a state of emotional turmoil, staring sightlessly at the model rockets suspended from the ceiling above him. If he kissed Laura, she'd never speak to him again. If he didn't, the guys would put it all over school that he lacked the guts to do it. Then they'd be calling him a wimp instead of Lover Boy.

I wish I'd never started this. Maybe I could hint to Laura that she should sit on the other side of the room tomorrow. I couldn't kiss her then.

Ryan lay awake half the night worrying over it. Whose opinion meant more to him, Laura's or his pals'?

"You look like you've had a hard day's night," said Matt as they walked into school together.

"Couldn't sleep. I can't do it. That *would* be a cheap shot."

"Laura isn't one of my all-time favorite people, but this time I agree with you. I don't know what got into those guys, but Peter sure is out to get Laura for something. Want me to put her wise?"

Ryan shook his head. "That wouldn't be fair. I got myself into this jam; I'll have to get myself out."

"Let me know if you change your mind."

"Hi, Ryan," said Laura brightly when he walked

32

into trig. He had to pass her desk to get to his. "All the thorns are still intact this morning."

"Great," he mumbled, scarcely looking at her.

He stalked to his place in the back of the room, between Matt and Jason, ignoring Laura when she turned around to look at him. Maybe if he were unfriendly enough, she wouldn't want to sit beside him in English.

"The girl is primed," whispered Jason. "She'll probably faint from joy."

Ryan gave him a cold look. "I don't think she'd like it at all."

"Chickening out?" taunted Jason.

Mr. Tuxford called the class to order, which gave Ryan an excuse to ignore his tormentor.

I could come in late from physics, after they've already started reading, thought Ryan. *No, Laura might save me a seat next to her.*

He arrived in English first. Maybe they wouldn't finish the play today. The kiss didn't come until the last page. Laura came in carrying an orange gym bag and noisily plunked it down on her desk, then turned to him with a bright smile. It made him feel even worse.

"Have you read the scenes for today?" she asked.

"Yeah. We don't have many lines together."

"Not too many. I'll leave you to challenge my enemies to battle like a true knight in shining armor. I think it's kind of romantic that men would actually fight a duel for a lady's honor. Of course, from a practical point of view, I'd rather have a live coward than a dead hero. I don't think Beatrice ever considered that."

Ryan's stomach fluttered nervously. Okay, if he

33

took her at her word, he'd drop the idea of the stupid dare. Yet if he didn't follow through, his pals, Peter in particular, would never let him hear the end of it.

Mrs. Kingsley had them push their chairs into a circle while she took roll. For a moment Ryan hoped Laura would sit on the other side of Matt. She calmly positioned her chair next to his, then opened her gym bag. She took out a heavy pair of hockey gloves and a goalie's helmet, complete with full face mask. Putting them on, she turned toward Ryan.

"Just in case you get carried away with your part again," she said in a muffled voice.

Ryan leaned back, grinning from ear to ear. "David didn't dress up like that when he went out to face Goliath."

"Goliath didn't have a reputation as a red-hot lover. Admit it, Lover Boy, I won this round."

Chapter 3

Ryan thoroughly enjoyed that class. When he came to the line, "Peace! I will stop your mouth," where he was supposed to kiss Beatrice, Laura obligingly leaned toward him and offered the side of her mask. Ryan kissed it amid the cheers and laughter of the class.

"You're one smart lady," he said, grinning happily while they put back their desks.

"You should have known I wouldn't give you the chance to get funny two days in a row."

"I'm glad you didn't," he said aloud, then added to himself, *You'll never know how glad!*

Ryan helped her pack everything back into the bag, then gallantly carried it to her locker for her. The way Laura was smiling at him now, he didn't care what Peter or Craig or Jason might think. He enjoyed sparring with her and he didn't want to be on the outs with her.

Ryan helped her on with her jacket, then offered to carry the gym bag out to the bus for her.

"Thanks, but I can handle it." She dazzled him with another smile that set his heart fluttering. "You know, I'm kind of sorry we finished that play. I was really beginning to enjoy it."

"So was I. Even if you did sound like you were reading your lines from inside a goldfish bowl."

"There's more than one way to defeat the enemy. See you tomorrow."

Ryan watched her join another girl and walk down the stairs. He sighed to himself. One of the boys from English passed and punched Ryan's arm playfully.

"So that's why they call you Lover Boy. You never miss a chance. I'm not sure I would have tried it with Laura."

"It's no fun without a challenge." Ryan made his way through the rapidly emptying halls to his locker. He felt a mixture of relief and elation. *That was a close shave. I don't ever want to get in a mess like that again.*

Matt was leaning against the locker bank, waiting for him. "So what do I do with the ten bucks now?"

"Give it back to those guys and tell them to shove it!" Ryan sighed heavily. "When Laura put that dumb mask on, I could have kissed her out of pure relief! Did you clue her in on what was up?"

"It was all her idea. That's her brother's hockey gear so she had to bring it from home. I didn't see her until trig."

"In all the years we've been arguing, I've never been as happy to lose as I was today. Sometimes that girl is out of sight."

Matt gave him a peculiar look. "Do you like her?"

"Yeah, but just as a friend. You can't help admiring a girl with a sense of humor like that."

At that moment, Peter, Craig, and Jason converged on them. Matt reached for his wallet to return their money.

"We heard what happened," began Peter. He looked

36

more annoyed than if he'd lost the money. Ryan wondered why.

"It's a draw," said Ryan quickly. "The bet was to kiss her on the mouth, not a plastic mask."

"She really sat through the whole class with that thing on?" asked Craig.

"Mask, helmet, and gloves. She wasn't taking any chances," Ryan assured him.

Jason shook his head, disbelief plain on his face. "I'm surprised old lady Kingsley didn't tell her to take it off."

"I'm not," said Matt. "She knows what the play is and she didn't think it was too funny yesterday when Ryan kissed Laura's hand."

"So the Libber wins again," said Peter, sounding peeved. "I've got to hand it to her, she never misses a chance to put a guy down."

Ryan looked at him sharply. "She wasn't putting me down. She outsmarted me. It would have been a lot easier for her just to sit on the other side of the room. It was a class move—I only wish I'd thought of something that good."

The story was all over school by the next morning. Ryan endured some good-natured kidding in all his classes. He wasn't sure but he suspected Eric Van-Bruggen sounded a little jealous. Was he the one who took Laura to the Sweetheart Formal? Ryan wished he could remember. Eric could be a troublesome rival.

Rival? Jeez, you'd think I liked Laura. Or that she liked me. I wonder if she'll smile much at me now that we've finished that play.

During lunch, Ryan noticed Peter looking at him as if he were still sore. If Peter didn't like losing, he shouldn't have pushed Ryan into the stupid bet in the first place. One of these times when they were alone, he'd ask Peter just what the problem was.

He finished lunch ahead of the others and told them he was going out to get a little air. The combined smells of chili, hot dogs, sauerkraut, and pizza were overpowering today. Why couldn't the cafeteria ever smell good?

"Air or meet Laura?" kidded Craig.

"Knock it off," snapped Ryan. "Laura is just somebody I argue with, okay?"

He dumped his styrofoam plate and milk carton into the trash barrel by the exit to the quadrangle. A moment later, he pushed through the double glass doors, ignoring a taunt behind him. The joke was definitely wearing thin.

While he was trying to sort out his feelings about Laura, Therese sauntered up, dressed in Hawaiian print shorts and crop top. She assumed a provocative posture against the brick wall. This time he wasn't particularly glad to see her. She gave him one of her suggestive smiles.

"I'll bet you were relieved to see Laura put on that mask yesterday."

"Yeah." Something about the way she said it offended him. He didn't need another person cutting down Laura.

"*I* wouldn't have worn a mask."

Ryan thawed a little. "I wouldn't mind kissing you."

"It would be pretty boring kissing little Miss Goody Goody. She probably doesn't even know how. I'll bet she hasn't had three dates in her whole life."

"Hey, it's over. Can we just drop the subject? I don't want to spend the rest of my life hearing about it."

"You don't have to bite my head off!" said Therese, miffed. "I certainly don't care who you kiss."

She flounced off, leaving Ryan standing there with a grim look on his face. Why had he ever thought kissing Therese was so great? Half the guys in town—not just the school—had kissed her. Ryan was sorry now that he'd been one of them.

Ryan suddenly realized he also regretted the Lover Boy nickname. Mom had had a fit when Cheryl mentioned it the first time. Dad laughed it off as a "boys will be boys" kind of thing. Ryan later promised Cheryl a very short life if she ever brought it up again.

"You have a fight with Therese?" asked Matt, interrupting his thoughts. He brushed gravel off the top of the wall before hoisting himself up to sit on it.

"Not exactly. She said some things about Laura that I didn't like. I'm getting a little fed up with the way everybody cuts Laura down."

"Not everybody does. A lot of kids think she was pretty clever to come up with that mask idea."

Ryan kicked at a pebble irritably. "The whole thing's my fault. I shouldn't have started it. Next time Laura tells me to get out of something, I'll listen to her."

Matt gave him that peculiar look again. "I think she wanted you to get out of it because it hit too close to the mark," he said slowly. "I think she really does like you and pretends she doesn't to keep anybody from guessing the truth, just like in the play."

"You're nuts!" said Ryan, a little too vehemently.

"Yeah? Ask her out and see what happens."

Ryan found himself thinking that wasn't such a bad idea.

The next few days, Ryan found himself watching Laura for clues that she liked him. If Matt thought so, and Laura blushed when he hinted at it in her kitchen, maybe there was something to the idea. Her eyes seemed to sparkle a little more whenever she looked at him. Or was he imagining things?

This is crazy, just like that stupid play when they tried to make Benedick think Beatrice loved him. Laura wouldn't go out with me on a dare. She really looked pretty in that blue dress she wore today. It was perfect with her blue eyes. And she has a good sense of humor.

It struck Ryan that Laura's sense of humor was one of the things he liked best about her. Not many girls he knew could laugh at themselves the way Laura did.

Thursday afternoon, when the last test was turned in, Mrs. Kingsley told the class they could talk for the few remaining minutes. Laura turned around to ask Ryan's help with a trig problem. He patiently showed her how to work it out, step by step. Laura watched as intently as if he were transforming lead into gold. Suddenly her face brightened.

"I think I got it. Are all the rest of them the same formula?"

"Right. Now you do it for me."

Laura went through each step the way he'd showed her. Ryan wondered if she always bit her lip like that when she concentrated. There he was, looking at her lips again instead of following her pencil.

He could smell her flowery fragrance again. A nice, clean smell. Lily of the valley—Mom had a patch by the back patio that always scented the whole backyard. It suited Laura.

He became aware of her mumbling and strained to

hear the words. Laura couldn't really be cursing out the trig book. It struck him funny. Suddenly, a light seemed to go on. The delighted smile she gave him when she actually got the problem made his heart do a little flop.

"It worked!"

"Sure it worked. Didn't you know I'm a genius?"

She sighed heavily. "I'm not. I don't know why I ever signed up for trig; my mind is a closed door when it comes to higher mathematics."

"I feel the same way about this Shakespeare stuff."

Laura closed her book and put it back on her desk. "You could understand Shakespeare even if you didn't like it. I feel like I'm in a constant fog in trig."

"I take it you're not going to be in calculus next year," said Ryan, grinning.

"No way! I made a deal with Mr. Tuxford. If he passes me with a C, I'll never darken the doors of the math department again. I've satisfied the college requirements and convinced even my father than I'm not suited to a career in the sciences. He's an optician and thinks I should be, too."

"Maybe we'll have some other class together then. I'd hate to go through a whole year without a chance to score a major victory over my favorite enemy." He *didn't* want to go through a year without her. She was part of his life.

"There is such a thing as defeat with honor. It's all a matter of recognizing the superiority of your foe."

"I might call my foe a lot of things but superior isn't one of them. You're a throwback to the sixties. Who cares about women's lib now?" said Ryan, laughing.

Laura sniffed, watching him with impish eyes.

41

"You dedicated male chauvinists would rather bury your head in the sand than accept the fact of woman's natural superiority. Just because feminists aren't as visible now, you think it's all blown over."

"I suppose you think you could set me straight."

"Watch it, Ryan," said Matt. "Remember what happened the last time you tangled with Super-Libber."

"She can't win them all. Tell you what, I'll give you a fair chance to state your case Friday night."

Laura reluctantly shook her head. "Much as I'd welcome the opportunity to enlighten your misguided mind, I'm going to a party Friday night."

"How about Saturday," persisted Ryan. "Or are you going steady with somebody?"

He hoped she said no. Why hadn't he ever thought of that possibility before? Maybe that's why VanBruggen acted so ticked off this morning.

"No steadies." She hesitated, her eyes becoming sober. "If you're asking me for a date, I'll give you my phone number and you can call me at home."

"What's wrong with right here? A simple yes or no; you don't have to make a big deal of it," said Ryan, aware that he now had an audience. Why couldn't people mind their own business?

"Because it isn't a simple yes or no, and I'd rather not talk about it with half the class listening."

Common sense told Ryan to drop the subject but pride wouldn't let him. He'd asked her out and if she didn't want to go, all she had to do was say no. He didn't want anybody asking him later what she'd said. He made a last attempt to save face.

"Hey, if you have to ask your mother, I can call you tonight. No problem."

For a moment Laura looked as if she wanted to brain him with her trig book. She kept her voice low and steady. "I don't have to ask my mother. I'm a big girl now; I decide for myself who I do or don't want to date."

"And you don't want to date me," said Ryan petulantly, raising his voice.

"That's the whole problem, Ryan, I *do* want to date you. I think we might have a good time together. Call me tonight and we can talk about it."

"We can talk about it right here and now. You want to go out with me and you think we'd have fun. So what's the problem?"

He met Laura's glare with one of his own. She clenched her jaw, as if determined not to say another word. It only added to Ryan's irritation.

"I want an answer, Laura."

"Then lean forward so I can whisper it. I don't want the whole world to hear me."

His heart sank. It must be pretty bad if she couldn't say it out loud. Why did he have to be so stubborn? Ryan stretched across his desk, lowering his head to Laura's level. The touch of her hand cupping his ear and her warm breath sent a strange thrill through him. And that perfume filled his nostrils.

"I'd like to accept but I *don't* want to be known as one of Lover Boy's girls. If I went out with you, that's exactly what I'd be called. I don't need that kind of a reputation. I don't think half those stories about you are true, but my brother's been talking about you all week and my mother *does* believe it."

Ryan flushed a deep red, his embarrassment accented by his fair coloring. He drew back, acutely conscious of the curious stares of the other kids. Leave it to honest Laura to lay it on the line.

"I'm sorry I embarrassed you, Ryan," said Laura softly. "I didn't want to."

"My fault. One of these days I'm going to learn how to pay attention when you tell me something."

The dismissal bell saved them from any further awkward moments. It took every ounce of will power Ryan could muster to keep from running out of class.

Matt tactfully avoided the subject while they stored their books in their lockers. Ryan's face still felt warm. Without looking at Matt, he repeated Laura's words.

"You know, Laura usually doesn't care what people say about her. If she's worried about the reputation she'd get dating me, I must really be the pits," he said despondently.

Matt gave him a sympathetic look. "Hey, don't put yourself down. Laura said she didn't believe the stories, so it's her mother who's the problem."

"Okay, Laura might take a chance. But if she can't go out with me, there probably isn't a nice girl in school who will. I thought being called Lover Boy was so cool!"

Ryan couldn't get the incident out of his mind. It nagged him all through work. Even Mom's special spaghetti sauce lost its flavor. After playing with his food for several minutes, he returned the plate to the oven.

"I think I'll go for a run," he said, popping his head into the family room. "Maybe work up an appetite."

His father glanced up from his paper, plainly surprised. "When did you ever need to work up an appetite?"

"Now," said Ryan curtly. "Be back in a while."

He quickly changed into shorts and T-shirt, then traded his loafers for Adidas. A few stretching exer-

44

cises and he took off out the back door, headed toward the park.

I thought only girls had to worry about a bad reputation. And Laura thinks she'd have one if she went out with me. Or at least her mother does. Why didn't I set the record straight when Therese started that dumb Lover Boy stuff? Then I had to show off with those other girls I dated this year, really impress them with my hot kisses. I thought it made me such a big man. Who cares about dating that little squirt anyway?

Ryan ran through the outskirts of the park, keeping clear of couples cuddling under the thick trees. Coming to the picnic area, he slowed down, then sat on one of the tables, breathing hard. After a few minutes rest, he veered toward Matt's house on the eastern side of the park.

Matt was vacuuming his car, a rusted but runable Capri. "Be with you in a minute, as soon as I clean under the floor mats. It's been about three months since the last crud removal."

"No rush." Ryan panted. "I need to catch my breath."

He followed Matt down the stairs of the modest ranch house to the basement bedroom Matt shared with his older brother, now at college. Ryan collapsed on the bottom bunk.

"Want a cold drink?" asked Matt.

"Not after running. Maybe later."

It was a comfortable room with clothes strewn about, not hopelessly tidy like Mom made him keep his room. Ryan lay there, staring at the upper bunk, trying to sort out his thoughts. Finally he rolled over on his elbow to look at Matt, seated in the desk chair.

"Therese said a lot of things that aren't true. We've never . . . you know. I thought about it a few times, but, well, I didn't want to risk it."

Matt nodded. "Yeah, I know Therese. She doesn't exactly *say* things; she just hints a lot. I think she likes being known as a hot number. With that babe, I'd worry about catching something, even with protection."

"I thought it was pretty macho being called Lover Boy, too—over nothing more than some hot kisses. I know this sounds crazy, but I like Laura. And I want her to like me."

Matt picked up a model plane and studied it carefully, avoiding Ryan's eyes. "I kinda thought you were drifting in that direction when you kissed her hand. You were too gentle for it to be a joke and too upset when she got mad."

Ryan groaned softly. "Do you think anybody else knows?"

"They do now. You two were lit up like the Las Vegas strip for a while this afternoon."

"What do I do now?" asked Ryan, rolling into a sitting position. "I can't walk up to Laura and tell her I haven't been involved like that with Therese. Or anybody else. She might believe me but her mother wouldn't."

Matt ran a hand through his thick hair. "I wish I knew what to tell you. I have trouble just trying to talk to a girl I really like. Regular girls are no problem, but the minute I start liking one, I can't say half a dozen words without getting all twisted up."

"That's the only good thing about having a sister; you get used to talking to girls."

"There's a girl in psych I'd like to ask out, but I'm not sure her father would let her accept. He's

46

real overprotective and hardly lets her date at all. Knowing that doesn't help when you're trying to work up the nerve to ask.''

Ryan nodded. "I know what you mean. Sweaty palms, dry mouth, pounding heart, and that's *before* you pick up the phone to call. And you don't even have a bad reputation.''

They sat there, glumly absorbed in their own thoughts for a few moments. Ryan picked at the quilted spread on Matt's bed. What made him stop thinking of Laura as somebody to argue with and now think of her as a possible date?

"What if I offered to help Laura with her trig? If we're doing homework in her house with her mom and dad right there, they shouldn't have to worry about her reputation. Maybe it would convince them I'm not such a bad guy."

"Good idea. Let me know if it works. I might try the same thing with Sue, only she'd be the one helping me."

"Laura can't do any more than say no. Again."

Ryan didn't get a chance to speak to her during trig. He made it a point to get to English early, hoping she'd also be early. She came in, stopping a minute to ask Mrs. Kingsley something. When Laura finally reached her desk, she put her books down, then, still standing, looked Ryan straight in the eyes.

"I had a long talk with Mom about you. If you're free Saturday night, you could come over and watch a movie on our VCR. We've got over a hundred to choose from."

Ryan smiled a little nervously. "Are you asking me for a date, Lady Disdain?"

"That's right. Girls in this school have been asking guys out for years. I'm just carrying on a time-honored tradition.''

She stood there, not batting an eye, daring him to refuse. She must like him if she'd made the effort to convince her mother he was okay. Being a debater gave her the inside track on winning arguments.

Ryan looked at that challenging smile, aware that they were once again the center of attention. He caught Matt's broad wink behind Laura. Leaning back in his seat, he regarded this assertive female with the saucy dark curls.

''Are your parents going to be home?'' he asked.

''Of course. They'll be in the front room. The VCR is in the family room.''

''Close enough so they can rush to the rescue if you scream for help.''

''Listen, Lover Boy,'' said Laura, putting her hands on his desk and leaning forward with mock menace, ''*nobody* has to come to my rescue. You try anything funny and I'll punch you out myself.''

Ryan grinned, then chuckled. ''I'm twice your size, Mighty Mouse. You'd have to climb a stepladder to reach my knee.''

''Oh yeah?'' Laura grinned impudently. ''Haven't you ever heard of the Battle of Wounded Knee?''

''Yeah. The Indians lost.''

''Wanna make a bet as to which of us comes into class next week wearing a blond scalp tied to her belt?''

''I haven't accepted yet,'' he reminded her. ''First you threaten my knee, now my scalp. I didn't know you were such a bloodthirsty little squirt.''

''I'm out to get your scalp, your knee, and all the rest of your chauvinistic carcass. Are you coming or not?''

"This is a big decision. I'll have to give it some heavy thought." The way Laura was smiling at him right now, he wouldn't care if she really did carry through on some of those threats.

"Think fast. The invitation self-destructs in ten seconds."

"I accept."

"I knew all that assertiveness training would pay off someday," said Laura with a satisfied grin.

She sat down, unaware of the victory signals exchanged between Ryan and Matt. The teasing of the kids around her didn't bother her a bit. When class was over, Ryan walked her to her locker.

"Why did you ask me in class instead of during lunch or after school?"

Laura gave him a pitying glance. "After publicly rejecting you yesterday, you deserved a chance to reject me in front of the whole class."

"Decent of you." Very decent, considering the way he'd treated her. "Can I give you a ride home?"

"Not tonight. I'm going over to Sue's. We're having a pajama party and I'm helping her get the food ready."

"Any guys coming to this party? I'd even go out and buy a pair of pajamas," Ryan said, grinning mischievously.

"No way. Mr. Zimmerman said if any boys came near the place, he'd call the police. This is strictly a girls' party."

"Matt and I could put on wigs and nobody would ever know the difference."

"I suppose Matt would tie little pink ribbons around that mustache he's been nurturing."

Laura tossed her jacket over her arm and took her

sleeping bag and a sky-blue nylon tote bag out of her locker. Ryan immediately relieved her of them.

"Let me carry those for you. That's too big a load for such a little girl."

"You're not going to succeed in your attempts to brainwash me with all these cracks about my size," she said flippantly. "I'm just as capable as you are."

Ryan pretended to be deeply wounded. "Here I am trying to be chivalrous and you accuse me of brainwashing you."

"Hmmff! Chivalry is just another attempt by man to keep woman in a state of subjugation. But it's a nice way. Do you have to get anything from your locker?"

"I have to put my books away. I'm at the other end of the hall, by the science department."

"Then I'll go with you. Any preference for what kind of a movie we see tomorrow?" She fell in step beside him.

"No Shakespeare. And no R-rated movies. You're too young to be watching such stuff," said Ryan.

"That's what Mom is always saying, but we have some R-movies she lets us watch, like *Animal House*."

"What's your favorite?"

Ryan stopped in front of his locker and put down Laura's things. Quickly spinning the combination, he slid in his books and took out his jacket. Though the afternoons continued to be warm, it was generally below fifty when they came to school, not unusual for southern Michigan.

"Comedies, mostly, like *Tootsie* or *Ruthless People*. And *Romancing the Stone*. I love it when he swings across on that vine, smack into the cliff."

"I should have known you'd like that one. Some

poor guy tries to help out a woman and you think it's funny every time he gets put down."

"That isn't it at all," Laura protested. "I loved him. Who wants a man who's always perfect? He didn't let failure stop him; he kept trying and he came back to her at the end."

"You know something, squirt, I think you're a big fraud. You just pretend to be liberated. At heart, you're a hopeless romantic."

"How about optimistic romantic," she said, leading the way down the stairs. "If I didn't have any hope, I'd never have dared ask you to come over tomorrow."

"No problem. I intended to invite myself over to help you with your trig homework."

"You did?"

"That's right. You didn't think I was going to take no for an answer, did you? People might get the idea I'm scared of you." He pushed open the door and held it for Laura.

"I wasn't too sure you wouldn't tell me no."

"I'm a sucker for a smooth line. Do you always threaten to maim your dates when you ask them out?"

"Every single one I've asked so far."

Ryan grinned. "Just how many have you asked?"

"Counting you?"

"Counting me."

"I think that brings it up to a total of one. That's Sue in the maroon Mercury over there."

Ryan put Laura's things in the back seat, then looked down at her, suddenly feeling shy. "When shall I come over?"

"Seven or seven-thirty." Two pairs of blue eyes

51

met, then Laura quickly averted hers. That look gave Ryan hope. "Thanks for carrying my stuff."

"Anytime."

He opened the door for her, nodding to Sue, who watched them with wide-eyed curiosity. Laura slid in. Ryan closed the door, touching her shoulder through the open window, reluctant to let her go. He slowly grinned, then winked.

"No masks this time, Lady Disdain."

Chapter 4

Ryan and Matt went skating that evening, then stopped at Shakey's for a pizza. In a booth near the front, they spotted Therese and Jeff Yarbrough. Therese was sitting so close to Jeff that they looked like they were joined at the hip. Ryan nodded and kept walking to one of the long tables in the rear. He made it a point to choose a seat that would keep his back to Therese.

They had arrived between the heavy business hours, after the supper crowd but before the after-the-show bunch. Ryan liked this time; it gave them a choice of where they wanted to sit. The aroma of baking pizzas filled the room while a plaintive Willie Nelson song sounded from the juke box.

"So what'll we have?" asked Matt, straddling the bench on the opposite side. "The special?"

"Anything but anchovies. We could keep it simple and just have pepperoni with double cheese."

"And a pitcher of Mountain Dew," added Matt.

They pooled their money and Matt crossed to the window to place the order. He returned with the pitcher of pop and two glasses.

"Pizza'll be ready in about twenty minutes. We're

number two eighty-three." He filled the glasses slowly, keeping the foam down. "So you and Laura are all set for tomorrow?"

"Yeah. Can you believe that girl, standing there in front of the whole class, daring me to turn her down?" Ryan grinned at the memory.

"Only Laura the Libber could pull that off. There isn't another girl in school who'd even have tried it. What do you think she'd have done if you said no?"

Ryan sipped his pop thoughtfully. "Depends. If I told her I had other plans, I think it would have been okay. If I refused just to get back at her, I don't think she'd ever speak to me again. Not as a friend, anyway."

"I'll give her credit for more guts than I have. If I'd been her, I'd have called you at home or asked some time when we were alone. I sure wouldn't do it in front of the whole class. I can't even get up the nerve to ask a girl over the phone." Matt tipped some of the crushed ice from his drink into his mouth, crunching it.

"Now that I think about it, I don't know why I asked in class. Anyway, she said I deserved a chance to reject her publicly after she rejected me. You've gotta respect a girl who'd do that. Sometimes that liberated act of hers really grinds me, then she does something like this and I think it isn't so bad."

Matt chuckled. "You'd better watch your step. I think she really would punch you out if you tried anything."

"I *know* she would." Ryan grinned. "Funny how different girls are, isn't it? When Laura draws the line, you know you'd better not cross it. With some girls, it's more like a dare to see how far you'll go."

"One thing about Laura, you always know exactly

where you stand. That makes dating a lot simpler. I hate it when a girl teases and you don't know whether she wants you to try something or if she's just leading you on."

"Yeah. I think that was our number." Ryan rose and crossed to the counter, returning with a pizza so hot that he had to hold it by the edges. "Forgot the napkins; be right back."

They split the pizza in half and attacked it from either side, strings of cheese wrapping around their fingers. Ryan counted the pieces of pepperoni subconsciously, then looked again and counted aloud. He glanced up at Matt.

"How many pieces of pepperoni do you think they could get on here if they covered the whole thing?"

"A lot more than they did. Whenever Mom makes pizza at home, she has edge to edge pepperoni. But it's like hamburgers, you know? The ones you make at home just aren't the same as McDonald's or Burger King."

As they were finishing, Peter, Craig, and Jason came in. They deposited themselves on either side of the table with Ryan and Matt.

"Hear Laura asked you for a date," began Peter.

Ryan looked him straight in the eyes, his voice cold. "That's only half the story. I asked her first . . . and if you're thinking of cutting her down, don't."

Peter's eyebrows shot up and a long whistle escaped his lips. "So that's how it is. When did she stop being your number-one target?"

"I'm not really sure," said Ryan quietly. "Maybe it was when she put on that dumb mask. That was classic. That's what's so neat about fighting with her; she doesn't do ordinary girl things, like sit there and cry."

"I don't think Laura knows *how* to cry," said Peter, then hastily added, "Sorry, not putting her down, just stating the facts."

Craig interrupted. "Did you guys hear there's a party going on at the Zimmermans'? All girls. We thought we'd cruise by and check out the action."

"Don't!" said Ryan abruptly. "Laura said Mr. Zimmerman would call the police if any guys showed up to hassle them."

"He doesn't need the police!" said Matt. "Have you ever seen him? He is one big dude. He used to be a lineman at Ohio State and he still looks like he could take on the Dallas Cowboys single-handed."

"How do you know, you check him out?" asked Jason. He stopped examining the meager contents of his wallet long enough to give Matt a curious look.

"They used to be on my brother's paper route. Sometimes I delivered it for him. When Mr. Zimmerman *requested* that Don put the paper in the door instead of throwing it in the yard, Donny did."

Craig made a show of stretching. "I guess the girls will have to get along without us. Their loss. What kind of pizza do you guys want?"

"It's almost ten," said Matt, looking at his watch. "If we're going to catch that movie on cable, we'd better be going."

"What is it?" asked Peter.

Broadcast News. Catch you later," said Matt.

The booth where Therese and Jeff had been sitting now stood empty. Ryan idly wondered when they'd left, then decided he didn't care.

A Ciera on the passenger's side of Ryan's VW was parked too close for Matt to open the door. He waited for Ryan to back out. Ryan expressed his opinion of the driver with a few salty words.

"You think those guys will go over to Zimmermans'?" asked Ryan, shifting from third to fourth gear. The traffic was light for a Friday night, but then they weren't on the usual cruise route the guys favored.

"If they do, they're idiots." After a silence of several moments, Matt asked, in a rather strained voice, "Is Laura a good friend of Sue's?"

"I don't know. Why?" asked Ryan, then glanced quickly at his chum. "Ah . . . Sue in psych. Sue Zimmerman?"

"Yeah. I'd kind of like to ask her to go to a movie or something, then I think about her father. I'm six-two and I have to look up to him."

"I'm bigger than Laura's father. Not that it matters." He stopped for a red light, drumming his fingers on the steering wheel. "Do you think she'd mind if I put my arm around her while we watched the movie?"

"Jeez, I don't know. I'm not sure I'd dare put my arm around Sue with her father a few feet away."

"I'm more worried about Laura than I am her father. I don't think I'll try to kiss her good night unless she kisses me first. Do you think she's that liberated?"

The light changed and Ryan slowly set the Bug in motion while Matt pondered his question. "I think I'd let her make the first move," Matt said at last. "If the porch light is on so all the neighbors can see you, I wouldn't kiss her."

"Good point. Jeez, I wasn't this nervous on my first date. I wonder if the other guys who dated Laura were this nervous."

Matt nodded, grinning. "Somehow I don't think

57

any guy's ever been one hundred percent confident around the Libber.''

Ryan was even more nervous about the date than he'd admitted to Matt. Several times at work Saturday, he actually found himself breaking into a sweat. Telling himself it was ridiculous to be that worried about a girl a foot shorter than he didn't help.

"Like saying concentrated TNT won't hurt you," he mumbled.

After supper, he showered and shaved—which he really didn't need—then rubbed on some of the Polo aftershave lotion Grandma had given him for Christmas. He thought the herbal pine fragrance would be a nice complement to Laura's floral scent.

Walking to his bedroom with just a towel around his waist, he tried to decide what to wear. Jeans? Too casual. He wanted to make a good impression on Laura's parents, even if it was just a date in their family room. Maybe his tan gabardine slacks. Should he wear a jacket or would that be too formal? While he stood staring at the closet, Cheryl walked in.

"Get lost, will you? I'm trying to get ready for a date."

Cheryl, a freshman in high school and going through a giggly stage, calmly plopped herself on the bed. Ryan glared at her, ready to call Mom to throw out the pest.

"I thought you could use some advice. Wear your navy poplin pants and blue-and-white-striped shirt. Blue is Laura's favorite color."

Ryan looked at her hesitantly, not sure she wasn't giving him a bad time. Who did she think she was to be offering him advice?

"I thought I might wear the tan pants with my camel sports coat."

Cheryl firmly shook her head. "That's more for going to the movies. Laura might feel funny if she's wearing pants instead of a dress. She'll probably wear her navy pants and that shirt with the little blue flowers. You'll be color coordinated."

Gripping his towel, Ryan turned all the way around to glare at his sister. She lounged on the bed, calmly swinging her foot back and forth, confident that she knew what she was talking about.

"How do you know what Laura likes?"

"Debate class, remember? She told us beginning debaters one time that it's important to wear clothes that give you confidence when you face a crisis. She used that outfit as an example of clothes that make her feel good."

Ryan grinned, relaxing. "Tell you what, if she wears that, I'll take you to Dairy Queen for one of their specials. Now get out of here so I can dress."

"One more thing," said Cheryl, pausing at the door, "don't put your arm around her until the movie's been running for half an hour. And don't try any clinches. She isn't Therese."

"I know she isn't Therese!" he snapped impatiently. Cheryl just looked at him. "I didn't mean to yell at you," he apologized.

"Yeah, I know—nerves. If she doesn't mind when you put your arm around her and she smiles a lot, it means it's okay to kiss her good night. If she keeps her distance, it isn't." With that, she left.

Ryan stared at the closed door, wondering how his fourteen-year-old sister knew so much about kissing etiquette. So far her dating had been restricted to group events.

Twenty minutes later, he turned into the Nettleton driveway, then immediately backed out and parked on the street. Four boys bounced around the driveway, shooting baskets at the hoop mounted above the garage door. All four stopped to stare at Ryan. He recognized Laura's brother Tim, a gangly boy in Cheryl's freshman class.

"Just what I needed, a welcoming committee," mumbled Ryan under his breath. He locked the car and pretended to a nonchalance he was far from feeling as he headed for the front door.

"Hi," said Tim. Laura's skinny brother might be younger than she but he was already half a head taller.

"Hi," Ryan replied. He felt as if he were walking a gauntlet. "I thought you were into hockey not basketball. What are you shooting?"

"I'm seven out of twenty-two. You're on the varsity team, aren't you?"

"Yeah. Eighteen was my game high for the season."

"I remember that game. It was against Ambledon and you had a free throw in the last three minutes that tied the game," said Tim excitedly. "Then Brett Jamison put in the winning basket."

Ryan grinned. He wished he knew if Laura had seen the game, too. Still, it was nice to have a fan. Maybe if he took the time to bs with Tim, it would soften the boy's harping on the Lover Boy image.

"If we'd won the next game, we'd have taken the conference title. It's been six years since Lockwood won the conference."

"You'll win it next year. Think you could show us a few shots?" All the boys now regarded Ryan with hopeful looks.

"Not tonight," interrupted Laura, appearing at the door. "I didn't ask Ryan over to coach you in basketball."

One look at Laura's navy pants and blue flowered shirt banished most of Ryan's nervousness. He made a mental note to get Cheryl the biggest hot fudge sundae they had at Dairy Queen.

Ryan winked at Tim. "One of these days I'll bring Matt Maddox over and we'll take on you and your buddies. Really smear you."

The boys all made derisive noises, loudly declaring they'd wipe up the place with the two varsity stars. Tim brashly offered to spot them ten points, doubled by one of his pals.

"I hope you're prepared to keep that promise," said Laura in a low voice when Ryan reached the door. "Tim will never let you forget it."

"I don't mind. Matt's big brother used to let us play basketball with him and his buddies once in a while."

Ryan greeted Laura's father, then she introduced her mother, a plumper version of Laura with a sprinkling of silver threads glistening in her dark hair.

"It's so nice to meet you at last," said Mrs. Nettleton. "We've heard so much about you over the years. I've asked Laura a number of times why she didn't invite you over."

Laura's face was getting pink again. Ryan casually reached for her hand and squeezed it.

"It's nice to meet you, too, Mrs. Nettleton. Just before I left, my mother wanted to know if she was ever going to meet Laura."

Having survived the encounter with Mrs. Nettleton, Ryan followed Laura into the family room on the lower level of the house. "Did your mother really say that or were you just being polite?'' Laura asked quietly as soon as they were out of earshot.

"She really said it. It turns out she and your mom were in the same aerobics class last fall and still meet once in a while at the walk-in center.''

Laura groaned. "Knowing my mother, they probably got together over coffee and planned out our whole future.''

"Do you mind?'' asked Ryan softly.

Laura looked up at him, then quickly looked away, her face once more suffused with color. "It's our first date. They don't have to start planning so soon.''

Actually, Ryan felt pretty good about it. With Mom on his side, maybe Mrs. Nettleton would be more likely to discount any stories she'd heard about him. He only wished he knew what her brother had told the family about his Lover Boy tag.

Floor to ceiling bookcases lined one wall of the family room with a section built in for the stereo, VCR, and television. Laura crossed to the shelves on the right of the VCR where numbered tapes rested behind glass doors.

Ryan glanced at the computer and printer in the corner. Judging from the layout and stack of papers, it wasn't used for games. "This your computer?'' he asked.

"Dad's mainly, but he lets Tim and me use it for school reports. No games. Sure beats typing.''

"I can believe that!''

"Here's the list of movies,'' said Laura, handing him two typed pages. "We've got a pretty wide selection, from the classics like *Casablanca* to the *Star Wars* series.''

"You know, I've always wanted to see *Star Wars*

and *The Empire Strikes Back* as a double feature. Do you think we'd have time?''

Laura glanced at the banjo clock mounted above the computer. "It's quarter after seven now. If we watched one right after the other, with no breaks, we'd be finished around eleven.''

"Let's go for it.''

Ryan watched while Laura loaded the cassette, then adjusted the monitor. "Do you have a VCR?'' she asked.

"Not yet. My sister and I have been trying to talk Dad into one but he says we need the money to repair the roof. We had a lot of damage from ice backing up under the eaves last winter.''

"I know what you mean. Dad and Tim went up on our roof a couple times last year to shovel off the snow, especially over the garage. Dad was afraid it would crack the timbers.''

Laura pushed the play button and motioned for Ryan to sit down. He took one end of the colonial print couch, leaving Laura a choice of the other end or sitting beside him. He certainly didn't expect her to sit in the rocker or recliner.

"Tell me when the volume sounds right,'' she said, twisting the knob.

"About there . . . no, back off a little . . . there. Are we going to leave all these lights on?'' asked Ryan, glancing from the recessed overhead lights to the lamp at the end of the couch. *Maybe I shouldn't have said that. I don't want her to get the wrong idea.*

"Just the lamp. Would you like a Coke or Sprite?''

"Coke . . . with ice, please.''

Ryan settled back to watch the prologue and initial attack on the space ship. Laura and Darth Vader made their entrances simultaneously. She placed a tray on the coffee table with two glasses of Coke, a bowl of Doritos, and a smaller bowl of salted nuts. Her hostess duties completed, she seated herself in the middle of the couch, about two feet from Ryan. Ryan stared at those two feet and took a chance.

"You can sit closer if you promise not to bite my ankles," he said, eyes twinkling.

She scooted a little closer, still leaving a discreet six inches between them. Ryan considered draping his arm across the back of the couch, then rejected it. If her parents "dropped in" throughout the evening, he didn't want them to have any reason for complaints. *Don't rush it and get thrown out.*

They watched the movie, contentedly munching on chips and peanuts, and had just gotten to the garbage dump scene when Tim came in and flopped down in the recliner. Laura immediately stiffened, ready to do battle. Ryan gave her hand a warning squeeze, leaning down to whisper in her ear.

"Let me handle this. Go refill our glasses and *don't* call your mother."

Laura shot Tim a look that would have done credit to Han Solo's blaster, then reluctantly left. When she was out of earshot, Ryan turned to Tim, who now looked at him with a mixture of curiosity and bravado.

"You don't have to worry about protecting your sister, Tim; I'm not going to try anything."

"You're sitting beside her. You have the whole couch." Tim's eyes were hostile, his chin aggressive.

"Laura sat beside me, but that isn't the point. I know how you feel. I've got a sister who's fourteen and if I saw you sitting close to her, watching TV, I might think I had to stick around, too."

"Nobody ever called me Lover Boy."

"Not yet. And I'll tell you something, you wouldn't like it if they did. I found out the hard way that isn't the kind of a reputation a guy wants. Nice girls like Laura won't go out with you. They stay home with their parents and brothers to protect them."

Tim blinked twice. "What a bummer."

"Yeah, it is. Sort of like being on probation. I have to watch movies in your basement until your family decides I'm trustworthy enough to take her out to a movie. You don't want that to happen to you."

"I sure don't." They locked eyes for a few seconds, then Tim got up and sauntered toward the door. "I know this movie by heart . . . think I'll go watch the one on upstairs."

Laura immediately returned with more Coke and a questioning expression on her face. Ryan gave her a conspiratorial wink.

"We had a man-to-man talk. I don't think he'll be back."

"He won't if he values his life!"

"It's all over now, so simmer down."

Laura placed the glasses on the coffee table, then glanced from Ryan to the TV. "Do you want me to back up the tape so we can see the part we missed?"

"Neat. I forgot you could do that with a recorder."

"We've got a fast forward or freeze frame, too. You can skip over the boring parts in a movie and just watch the parts you like. Tim likes all the battle scenes in these movies and I like the parts with Han and Leia."

"They were kind of like Benedick and Beatrice; first they just argued all the time, then they loved each other."

"It's a common theme in literature," said Laura. "Hate at first sight always turns into love."

"Always?" murmured Ryan, gazing into her eyes.

Laura blushed and abruptly jerked her head around, staring at the screen as if she'd never seen it before. He'd seen her blush more tonight than in all the years he'd known her put together. He wondered how long she'd liked him.

Ryan saw the tension gradually ease out of her body. By the end of the film, her head rested against his shoulder. He couldn't remember the exact moment they'd gotten that close; it just seemed to happen naturally.

"Do you want to take a break?" asked Laura, while she changed cassettes. "The bathroom is the second door on the left, next to the laundry room. And I could fix some hot dogs in the microwave."

"Sounds good." Ryan stood and stretched, his hands touching the acoustical tile of the ceiling.

"What do you like on your hot dogs? We've got mustard, ketchup, pickle relish, and chopped onions."

"The works," he said, then reconsidered. "Are the onions supposed to keep me at my distance, like the mask?"

"I can hold the onions if you'd like," said Laura, almost defiantly.

He shoved his hands in his pockets, grinning as he watched her. Tonight was turning out a lot better than he'd expected. Maybe he'd even get a chance to find out how soft and warm those pink lips really were. But only if she made the first move. He knew her remark about the onions wasn't an invitation, just a way to let him know she didn't need masks or onions to stay in control.

The film ended shortly after eleven. Ryan helped

Laura carry the dishes back to the kitchen, then said good night to her parents. Laura walked out to his car with him. Not only was the porch light on, floodlights blazed away from either side of the garage and a streetlight stood forty feet away. Ryan looked around and sighed heavily. He wondered how much of their illumination was Tim's doing.

"If you can kiss me in front of a whole class, you can kiss me in front of a few lights," said Laura softly.

He leaned against his car, hands jammed in his pockets, regarding Laura thoughtfully. "About that day in class . . ."

He swallowed hard, not sure he should tell her about the bet. If he didn't, she might hear about it from someone else. Ryan decided he'd rather have a chance to tell his version first.

Laura placed her hands lightly on his waist and looked up at him, her eyes almost a velvet softness. "I heard about the bet in trig class. Jason told Phil who told Marcy who told me. You were so unhappy, I knew you didn't want to do it. I already had the hockey gear in my locker. It saved us both a lot of embarrassment and got a big laugh."

"Way to go!" Ryan caught her in a bear hug, lifting her off the ground. "I wouldn't have done it, Laura, not for all the money in the world. I couldn't risk losing you."

"It's past history now and we've survived our first date. Almost." The expression in her eyes as she looked up at him was a mixture of hope and shyness.

Ryan gently brushed her lips. For such a quick kiss, it had his heart pounding. He even felt a little light-headed. "Thanks for a great evening. See you at school."

Laura laughed. "Some romantic you are. You're suppose to say you'll see me in your dreams."

"That's better than seeing you in my nightmares. I'm glad those days are over. Forever, I hope."

Chapter 5

Ryan's euphoria over his date with Laura evaporated when she came into trig late Monday, storm signals flying. She handed Mr. Tuxford her tardy admission slip and took her seat without a word. Ryan sat too far away to ask her the reason.

Matt nudged him. "You and Laura have a fight?" he whispered.

"No, this is the first time I've seen her today. I don't know what's wrong."

A horrible thought suddenly struck him—what if somebody had said something to her about dating him? His heart went to his feet. Therese? Could be. But why should she care if he dated Laura when she was dating Jeff?

Ryan had difficulty concentrating on trigonometric formulas. His gaze kept wandering to Laura, who kept her attention focused on the equations Mr. Tuxford was writing on the blackboard. The girl behind her finally gave up trying to find out what was wrong. Ryan wondered if Laura would have ignored him, too, if he were the one behind her.

Laura waited for him at the end of class. He wasn't sure whether it was defiance or because she really wanted to talk to him. Whatever the reason, he was grateful to see Matt "escort" Jason past her without stopping to talk.

"You in the mood to talk or shall we just walk?" Ryan asked quietly when he joined her.

"You can walk me to study hall. I'd rather have you hear this from me first." Her voice, though calm, sounded strained. "I was late because I was washing off the charming message someone wrote about us on the mirror in the second-floor girls' john."

"Want to tell me what it was?"

"That we spent Saturday night in bed together, but in four letter words." Her flushed face brought a few curious stares from kids passing them.

"I'm sorry—"

"Not your fault. I knew what I was getting into when I asked you over so publicly. I even warned my family there could be gossip. I didn't expect it to be quite so blatant. But I like you and I'm not going to let this change my mind."

"It wouldn't have happened if you hadn't dated me." His stomach churned painfully, adding to his stress.

Laura gave him a quick look, trying to smile. "Hey, some girl—or girls—is not happy that you actually accepted my invitation. They've never considered me as competition for a boy before, only as a candidate for school office, and they don't like it."

Ryan grinned ruefully. "Maybe it's because you've always won those offices."

"Right. Now they think I'm going to take you out of circulation, Lover Boy. They're trying to scare me off."

They came to the stairs and joined the mob trying

70

to go down against the mob coming up. Laura had once suggested a center railing be installed on the stairs for crowd control and was curtly told the school had no money for such things.

"If I ever find out who it was, I'll scare her off!"

"Don't let it bother you. I know that sounds dumb, as upset as I was an hour ago, but the shock has worn off now. Take my word for it, it's better to laugh it off than to go around trying to deny it or threatening to bash everybody."

He gave her a surprised look. "Laugh it off? I don't see anything to laugh about."

"Trust me; I've had a lot of experience with hecklers and verbal attacks. If you react, they get worse." She touched his arm, her voice becoming softer as she looked into his eyes. "Nobody really believes that stuff."

"They'd believe anything about Lover Boy," said Ryan bitterly.

Laura stopped walking and pulled him to one side. "Okay, so you've got a reputation for being a hot lover. I've got a reputation for drawing the line and sticking to it, come hell or high water. Do you honestly think the kids who know us and have seen us battling for years are going to think I suddenly fell at your feet, willing to let you try anything you wanted?"

Ryan grinned in spite of himself. "No."

"Okay. We can talk more about this at lunch. Right now you'd better get to history."

"Think I'll check out the boys' johns first. If there's anything written on those walls, we'll know it's more than one person. A girl sure wouldn't have been in there."

"That can wait until lunch. You know what a fit Colter has about tardies in his classes."

Ryan was even less attentive to the lecture on causes of the Korean War than he'd been in trig. Laura was probably right about playing it cool. That didn't mean he had to like the situation. He definitely didn't like seeing her take the brunt of the attack.

When he couldn't find her in the cafeteria, he wondered if she were inspecting the johns again. He hadn't found anything more than the usual graffiti in the boys' johns. Joining the gang, he knew by the way they initially avoided looking at him that they'd heard all about the graffiti in the girls' room.

Matt glanced at him sympathetically. "Laura okay now?"

"I wish I knew. She was supposed to meet me for lunch. Maybe she's scrubbing more mirrors."

Jason looked up from his lasagna. "Listen, good buddy, not everybody has it in for Laura. She's not on my top ten list but I don't think any girl deserves the kind of crap some sickie wrote about her and you. And I've yet to hear anybody who believed it."

"Thanks," said Ryan. "I still have trouble believing it happened. You don't expect kids in high school to do stuff that stupid. Nobody's ever once said anything about any of the other girls I've dated. At least, not that I know of."

"I've never heard anything," said Peter. He looked up, choosing his words carefully. "I know this isn't any of my business, but is Laura going to drop you now? I mean, she isn't used to people talking about her like this."

"She says no. *I'm* the one with the bad reputation." Ryan sighed, then took a vicious bite of his hamburger. "In the long run, it might make more

72

sense to ignore it than if I beat half the school to a pulp. Knowing that doesn't make me feel any better.''

Peter seemed to think it over for a long minute while he chewed his carrot stick. Finally he nodded. ''If anybody can stand the flack, it's Laura. She'll stick with you now just to prove a point, even if she dumps you later. No way would she ever let anybody get the best of her. She never has.''

That assessment left Ryan with mixed emotions. Maybe Laura could pull it off after all. But was she doing it because she liked him or to prove a point?

''You plan to back her up?'' asked Craig, then quickly added, ''I mean, you're not going to drop her to keep people from saying anything more?''

''I don't want to. I got her into this and I'll see it through. I just hope it doesn't get any worse.''

He caught a glimpse of Laura moving from the salad bar to the only empty table, near the entrance. Kids avoided sitting there because Mrs. Crawley, the school principal, liked to stand directly behind it during her visits to the cafeteria to make sure the student body was conducting itself in an ''appropriate manner.'' Food fights didn't happen in her cafeteria.

Laura must not have seen him. Picking up his tray, Ryan quickly maneuvered his way across the room to join her. He was surprised to find Matt close on his heels. They'd no sooner sat down than Jason and Craig joined them. A moment later, Laura's best friend Sue pulled out a chair opposite Matt. Laura looked from one grim face to another, then laughed.

''Hey, guys, it's not a public execution. It's nice to have my friends' support but I don't need body-guards.''

''I heard you were in Mrs. Crawley's office,'' said Sue. ''What happened?''

73

"Apparently stuff was written in all the girls' rooms and she saw it on one of her routine potty patrols. She had the custodians clean the mirrors I didn't get. Anyway, she wanted to know what was behind the attacks. I told her I didn't know, and I think I finally convinced her it was a personal matter, not worthy of her time."

Jason stared at her. "Did she buy it?"

"She said if it happens again, we'll have another talk. It's not so much what they said that's got her ticked off as the fact that they're writing on the mirrors. I'm only glad it was lipstick and not spray paint, like last year's graduating class used on the side of the building."

"She was not amused about that," Ryan said. "You know what a thing she has about people defacing school property. And the more she squawks about it, the more kids do it."

Laura grinned at him. "That's exactly the point I was trying to make with you this morning. If you ignore it, it might go away."

He gave her an answering grin. "Okay, you told me so. Not that Crawley hasn't got a point, too. Remember that idiot who threw a cherry bomb into one of the toilets a couple years ago and blew it off the wall? Or how about the Mad Slasher, after all the teachers' tires?"

"Ancient history," said Craig. "And they had to pay for the damage when they were caught. Or their parents did. Anyway, Crawley agreed with you?"

Laura finished her mouthful of salad before responding. "Believe me, telling Ryan was a piece of cake. It's kind of hard telling an adult—especially the principal—that she's going about the problem all wrong."

"But that didn't stop Laura the Libber," said Craig loudly. "Oh, no, not her, not ever."

"Watch it," snapped Ryan.

"Hey, I meant it as a compliment. Not even the superintendent has been able to get through to Old Hatchet Face that she should cool it. You'd think this dump was her own home the way she carries on when somebody does something to it. She has responsibilities, sure, but she doesn't have to go overboard."

Laura put up her hands, signaling them to be quiet. "Listen, guys, the way she's been acting is exactly what I don't want us to do. From now on, we act like it isn't worth our bother, okay?"

"If they don't get a rise out of you, they'll probably try something worse," pointed out Matt.

"Yeah, I know. The winner is who can hold out the longest. Frankly, I'm more worried about what my family will say. I only hope I get to my big-mouthed brother before he gets to Mom."

Ryan clamped his jaw. Whether Laura liked it or not, her parents might forbid her to see him again, and Laura would never sneak around behind their backs. And over nothing more than a video in her basement!

The warning bell sounded, ending lunch. Reluctantly, the group disbanded, dumped their plates, and carried their trays to the return window. Ryan noticed that Matt managed to get next to Sue, in case she needed any help with her tray. Nice to know somebody was benefitting from this mess.

A test in physics kept Ryan too occupied to worry, then came English class, with several kids wanting to know about their big date. Even Mrs. Kingsley seemed to be listening, though she'd never admit it.

"Really had a hot night, huh, Ryan?" taunted a boy from the back of the room.

Laura gave him a dazzling smile. "It wasn't hot—it was *torrid*. We generated enough heat to melt the polar ice cap. This was an orgy that would have made Caligula look like he was having a tea party. Wanna come over and watch the next time? We even supply popcorn."

Several kids laughed, while Ryan wished he could crawl through the floor. Laura just stood there, daring the jerk to say anything more. He backed off with a sheepish grin.

"Naw, I got better things to do with my time."

"Like open your book," said Mrs. Kingsley coolly. "I want you to have the first three chapters of *A Separate Peace* read for tomorrow. You may have this period to work on it, but if I see any of you doing other homework or fooling around, you'll get an hour-long lecture and do your reading at home. Everybody got that?"

A few voices mumbled assent, then the room fell silent. Turning pages, an occasional cough, or someone shuffling into a more comfortable position were the only sounds for the remainder of class.

Ryan stared at page one for a good five minutes before he actually saw any words. Chalk up another victory for Laura. Making Phillips look like a bigger jerk probably did shut him up faster than if Ryan had punched out his lights. He sighed, slowly relaxing.

When the dismissal bell rang, Laura turned to him. "Call me tonight if you have a chance. I'll let you know how things are on the home front. You'd better say something to your family, too."

"Right. Want me to take you home?"

"Much as I'd like to accept, it's in the opposite

direction from your job and I don't want you to be late for work. Talk to you tonight."

Ryan grinned. "You bet you will. About seven."

"That was quite a speech," said Matt. They ambled toward their lockers together. "Phillips knew he'd been burned."

"I'd never have thought of saying anything like that."

"Most people wouldn't, but then Laura has never been most people. Sometimes I think her mother must have OD'd on Don Rickles before Laura was born."

"She could have."

They dumped their books and headed for the exit, then their respective jobs. Ryan kept too busy at work to think much about the situation until just before closing when Jeff Yarbrough pulled in for a fill-up. Jeff stuck his head out his car window, craning to look back at Ryan.

"Heard you had a pretty hot date Saturday night with Laura the Libber. You plan to kill her with kindness now?"

Ryan tensed, then forced a smile. "Why not? I haven't gotten anywhere fighting with her."

"I think you made up the whole thing just to impress your buddies. I'll bet she made you sit on the opposite side of the room, with her whole family in between. Must be quite a shock after Therese."

Ryan decided to try Laura's tactics on Jeff. "You're right about the whole family. I mean *whole* family— her grandma and grandpa, sixteen aunts, nine uncles, and eighty-seven cousins. We had to take a number to use the john. But the worst part was when they made me kiss all of them good night before I could kiss Laura."

"You're full of it, Archer."

"You're the one who asked. Want your oil checked?"

"Don't bother." He handed Ryan a ten dollar bill and drummed the steering wheel in time to the song blasting on his stereo while waiting for his change. When he got it, he laid a strip of rubber gunning out into the street.

"Who does he think he's trying to impress?" muttered Ryan. Oh, well, when you didn't have to pay for your tires, you probably didn't care how much abuse they got.

His next customer was also one of the guys from school, notorious for the number of times he'd been suspended. He wanted two dollars' worth of gas. While Ryan manned the pump, Ben went inside to buy cigarettes. He paused outside the car to light up while Ryan returned the hose to the pump.

"The word's around that you're exploring virgin territory, Lover Boy. And you know something, not one guy has doubted that she is a virgin. Or should I say was?"

"Dominowski, I'm surprised you even know what a virgin is. In fact, I'm surprised you recognize any word that has more than four letters. Two bucks for the gas."

Ben dropped two singles on the cement. He deliberately blew smoke in Ryan's face, then got into his car. Though he tried, he couldn't get up enough speed from his rusty old clunker to lay rubber on the way to the road.

When Ryan went home half an hour later, he felt as if today had already been sixty hours long. Cheryl joined him while he ate his supper, uninvited and unwanted. Ryan didn't even waste breath telling her to get lost. She let him eat the first of his stuffed peppers in peace. When he started on the second, she hitched her chair closer and leaned her elbows on the table.

"Did Laura tell you what was written in the johns?"

"Not word for word, but I got the message." Ryan took a drink of milk, hoping she'd get discouraged and leave, even though he knew better.

"Want me to tell you?"

"No. Did you see it or just hear about it?"

"Saw it. Laura came into the second-floor girls' john just as I was getting ready to leave, so I waited to see what she'd do." Cheryl then shut her mouth, knowing curiosity would compel him to ask.

"And?"

"She just looked at it, said, 'What a waste of lipstick,' and used the john, then she left. Some of the other girls laughed about it, but it didn't sound like a real laugh, you know what I mean?"

"Yeah, I know. She said she was late for trig because she scrubbed it off." Ryan found his appetite fading fast and wondered if he'd even be able to get his salad down. Cheryl *could* have waited until he finished. "Come to think of it, why didn't *you* clean it off?"

"There weren't any paper towels in the holder and it would have taken all day with those little squares they put in the stalls for toilet paper. Laura must have gotten some towels from one of the other johns to clean it off."

Ryan looked at his salad, then thought of what Laura had said about not letting it get to him. Not even his "helpful" sister. He grimly reached for the dressing and nearly drowned the lettuce. After spooning off half the blue cheese, he picked up his fork

79

and slowly ate, taking out his frustration on the crunchy vegetables.

Cheryl ignored the fact that he was ignoring her. She waited until he'd finished eating before firing her next shot. "Some kids on the bus were talking about you and Laura real loud. I told them it couldn't possibly be true because Tim watched the movie with you."

Ryan closed his eyes, groaning softly. Leave it to Cheryl to make things worse when she thought she was helping. She sat there, watching him expectantly, waiting for a word of praise.

"Listen, dipstick, telling people Tim was there makes it sound like I'm either a wimp or a sex maniac. Do me a favor and don't do me any more favors, okay?"

"I was only trying to help." She sounded genuinely hurt.

"Okay, you meant well. But let me and Laura handle this. If you stick your nose in it, the next time it might be your name on the walls."

Cheryl glared at him. "How could it? I'm not allowed to have a boyfriend yet. All the other girls in my class—"

"No, not all the other girls in your class can date, so don't start in on that again, and I'm not the one who's stopping you anyway." Ryan picked up his glass, then set it down, giving Cheryl a penetrating look. "Did you tell Mom about this?"

"I left that for you. She'd just start asking a million questions and drive me crazy because I don't know the answers."

"Yeah." Ryan knew she was right. As soon as he found out how Laura fared, he'd have to tell his parents.

While Cheryl went in search of a sympathetic friend, Ryan rinsed his dishes and put them in the drainer. Carrying the phone into his bedroom, he locked the door, then dialed Laura's number. Mrs. Nettleton answered. She didn't sound mad or hang up on him. Maybe Laura hadn't told her yet.

Ryan plumped up the pillow and leaned back on his bed, waiting for Laura to answer. Maybe he should have gone over to her house instead. Why hadn't he thought of that sooner?

"Hi, Ryan," said Laura. They exchanged a few pleasantries, then Laura got down to business. "Like the old joke says, I've got good news and bad news. The good news is, Mom and Dad think I made the right move in not making a big fuss about it. They agree it's best to let it blow over. You don't know how glad I am that they're not the kind of parents who go charging into school, demanding somebody's head because their poor, innocent child has been slandered."

"I know how glad I am," said Ryan fervently. "What's the bad news?" He held his breath, hoping she wouldn't say she couldn't date him again.

"We have to keep having at-home dates until this blows over, which may mean the end of the school year. But that's only seven more weeks."

Ryan slowly expelled his breath. It could have been worse. "What about the prom? That's only four weeks off. I'd like to take you, if they'll let you go."

What made him think of the prom when he was already in a bind for cash? He'd have to find a way to swing it.

"I hadn't thought of that." She was silent for a moment. "I'm sure they'd let me go, but we'd prob-

81

ably have to come home right after it's over, not go on to any parties.''

"I wouldn't mind missing the parties as long as we could go to the dance." Ryan quickly shifted the phone to his other ear. "You can tell them about all the teachers and parents who chaperone.''

"That's true. It's not like going to some dimly lit disco or even a dark movie.''

"Speaking of movies, I guess I'll be coming over to watch another this weekend. Shall we offer to videotape us watching a videotape for the next loudmouth?''

Laura giggled. "We should. I have to get off the phone so Mom can make some calls. See you at school.''

"What happened to 'See you in my dreams'?''

"That was my line. Think up one of your own. Bye.''

Ryan returned the phone to the kitchen, then popped his head in the family room. Mom sat on the couch doing some cross-stitching and Dad was asleep in front of the TV. No sign of Cheryl. Now was probably as good a time as any to say something, before the prime-time shows started. Ryan sidled into the room, taking the opposite end of the couch.

"Uh . . . Mom," he began, his stomach fluttering a bit, "something happened at school today and I'd like your advice about it.''

She looked up, startled, one hand poised above her work, needle in attack position. "You want my advice? What happened? You didn't get suspended, did you? No, you couldn't have; Mrs. Crawley would have called home. Are you in trouble? Or flunking your classes?''

Cheryl was right about the million questions. "Not

exactly trouble. Not with teachers, or anything like that.''

As quickly as he could, considering the number of interruptions for more questions, he explained the situation, starting with his asking Laura for a date. By the time Ryan finished, Dad was awake, listening quietly. He switched off the TV with his remote control, then turned to Ryan. "I think your girl has the right idea. Don't add fuel to the fire by making a big ruckus about it. And having dates at her house is going to save you the money you need for that car insurance.''

Ryan grimaced. The way Dad said it made him feel cheap, as if he couldn't afford to take Laura out. Well, he couldn't, but Dad didn't have to rub his nose in it.

"I might take her to the prom, if her parents will let her go.''

"Fine, just don't ask me for any loans. Or your mother.''

"I'll talk to Nancy the next time I see her at aerobics,'' said Mom. "No, I'll call her. I don't want her thinking my son isn't good enough for her daughter.''

"Mom, she never once said that,'' argued Ryan hastily. "You know I've got this dumb nickname and they're worried about Laura's reputation. It's like you are with Cheryl; they want to be sure who their daughter is seeing.''

That calmed Mom a bit. "Yes, I see your point. I still think I'll have a talk with her.'' She turned to Dad. "I told you that name would cause him trouble!''

Ryan retreated to his bedroom. That name was causing him trouble all right. Was it really worth it to date a girl who'd spent five years sticking verbal pins in him?

"Yeah, it is," he mumbled. "Faint heart never won fair lady, as Shakespeare would say. Or was it somebody else?"

Chapter 6

Ryan found out it wasn't over yet when he arrived in his first-hour class the next morning. The three guys who sat around him waited until he was seated before starting in.

"How's it going, Lover Boy? You have another hot date with Laura last night? When you get a combination like Laura the Libber and Lover Boy, things happen."

"They sure do, VanDyke. Laura does her dance of the seven veils and I put on an act better than all the Chippendales put together. You really ought to catch it sometime. We let our friends see the show for half-price."

The burly wrestler across from Ryan laughed, turning to his pals. "Can't you just see Laura doing a striptease? She'd give you an hour-long lecture with each piece she took off. It would take hours before she even got to her shoes."

"You guessed it," replied Ryan. "It makes for a pretty long evening; by the time she's through, my curfew's come and I have to go home."

"So why'd you suddenly take up with her?" asked VanDyke. "I thought you spent all your time arguing with her."

"Still do. I've just left the skirmishes and moved on to a major campaign."

"Hey, hey, hey," crowed Stan, the wrestler. "That's what I said, you were playing it cool until you got her out on some dark road alone."

Ryan was saved from further harrassment by the bell. He sagged momentarily in his seat. It was just eight o'clock and he had a full day to get through. Laura's way might be better in the long run, but right now he'd like the satisfaction of one good punch.

Therese deliberately caught up with him between study hall and trig, slipping her arm around him. "Undue familiarity" was another of Mrs. Crawley's prohibitions. Ryan tried to ease away.

"What's the matter, Lover Boy?" she teased. "Worried people might start writing sexy things about us? Come over tonight and I'll make sure they have something to write about. Satisfaction guaranteed. I'll be home all alone."

They'd reached Mr. Tuxford's room by then and Ryan was chagrined to see Laura coming from the opposite direction. Therese saw her, too. She pulled his head down for a long kiss on the mouth. Furious and embarrassed, Ryan pushed her away. Therese favored Laura with a triumphant smile before she sauntered off.

"Don't you ever do that again," Ryan yelled after her. He made a vicious swipe across his mouth with the back of his hand. Laura silently handed him a tissue.

Therese laughed. "I didn't want you to forget what a real kiss was like. Miss Perfect certainly doesn't know how. She'd have to study diagrams."

Laura smiled sweetly at her. "I give lessons in private, dear. And he doesn't wipe them off." She pushed Ryan through the door before he could say more. "If you really want to stop her from pulling any more of those cute little tricks, the next time she kisses you, make some very loud remark about bad breath."

Ryan walked to his seat not entirely sure that the person who decided on co-educational schools made the right choice. He felt like the rope in a tug-of-war, Therese burning hot on one side and Laura freezing everybody with her voice on the other.

The leer Jason gave him did nothing to restore his good humor. "Hey, Lover Boy, what's it feel like to have two girls fighting over you?"

"One more crack out of you, Pringle, and you're going to find out what it feels like to eat a hamburger with no teeth," growled Ryan.

For the rest of the day, Ryan was on the alert for Therese. Laura didn't mention the incident at lunch, which left him wondering if she were mad, jealous, or indifferent.

In English, she seemed a little cool. Jealous, or had she been having a hard time all day, too? Kathy, a girl two rows over, tossed a paperwad at Laura to get her attention when Mrs. Kingsley stepped out of the room for a minute.

"Hey, Laura, I got a bet with Carrie Miller that you're the one who's been writing all that stuff. Now that Lover Boy's taught you how, you're advertising, right?"

Ryan's face reddened, but before he could say anything, Laura was giving Kathy one of her sweet smiles. "I'm so glad you approve. Who read it to you?"

"Whatta ya mean, who read it—oh, being funny. Ha, ha."

"There are two kinds of people in the world, the wits and the half-wits. You can always tell the half-wits; they're the ones who have to have jokes explained to them."

"Fight your battles on your own time, Laura," said Mrs. Kingsley, returning with some dittoes. "And that goes for the rest of you, too. Here are your study guides for the next three chapters. Now, what did we learn yesterday about interpersonal relationships from the first three chapters of our story?"

Mrs. Kingsley kept them too busy for any more insults. At the end of class, Laura asked Ryan if he'd mind coming over that evening to help her with her trig.

The dejected droop of her shoulders inspired Ryan to try kidding her out of it. He stepped all the way across the hall before answering. "If I do, you have to write 'Men Are the Superior Sex' ten times."

"Only in trig. In all other forms of human endeavor, they're still in the primordial soup."

"So you're going to be difficult, huh? I just might show you the problems in invisible ink."

"Then I'll have to whip out one of my magic incantations to make it reappear." She got close enough to step on his toes, though she didn't put down her weight.

"I'll bet you don't know magic incantations."

"I do. Chocolate mousse cake. Brownies a la mode. Strawberry shortcake."

Ryan rested his free hand lightly on her waist. "Okay, you know the magic words. Do me a favor?"

"Anything for you, sweet Benedick."

"Matt kind of likes Sue. Having her sitting beside him at lunch made him about one thousand percent more in favor of supporting you. Could you *subtly* find out what she thinks of him?''

Laura laughed delightedly. ''I don't have to. When we had the pajama party at her house, she kept bringing the conversation around to Matt, no matter what we were talking about. She also thinks Matt is sexier than Tom Cruise.''

''Matt would go through the ceiling if he could hear her say that! I don't suppose she's liberated enough to ask him out.''

''Fat chance! Her father would kill her.'' Laura caught his hand and dragged him toward his locker. ''You'd better get to work before you're late.''

''Hey, thanks for not making a big deal out of the thing with Therese this morning. And Kathy. And anybody else who's been on your case today.''

Laura smiled. ''Don't mention it. And I mean that.''

He felt almost ebullient during the drive to the station. Laura hadn't hassled him about Therese, and she'd asked him to come over tonight. Maybe things would work out after all. At least nobody had written on the walls today.

A different shock greeted Ryan when he arrived at the gas station. Mr. Dennison stopped him before he could put on his overalls. Ryan waited patiently while the older man dropped some change in the cash register, blew his nose, and finally sat down.

''I'm afraid I'm going to have to let you go.''

''What! Why?'' Ryan stared in disbelief. ''What did I do? I've been late only three times since I started.''

''Nothing you did, nothing at all. I just can't afford to keep you on. Business hasn't been as good as it used to be. Guess people would rather go to those serve-yourself places and save a few cents."

"Oh. Well, I'm sorry."

"I'm sorry, too, son. I made out your check for an extra week's pay." He handed it to Ryan, who accepted with a mumbled thanks. "If business picks up during the summer, I'll give you a call."

Outside, Ryan swore softly. Standing in the fresh air and sunshine, the world looked so bright and his future so dark. He couldn't afford to wait around for the business to pick up again. When had it dropped off? Ryan could have sworn it had been getting better all spring. Maybe they only had business during the evening when people were on the way home for work.

Realizing he'd accomplished nothing by hanging around the station, he drove more recklessly than his custom. *I've gotta find another job, fast. My car insurance comes due next month and I'm still short forty bucks. If I have to borrow from Dad, he won't let me drive the car until I pay him back. I've gotten that message loud and clear. On top of that, I asked Laura to the prom.*

Instead of going directly home, he stopped by Laura's house first. Since her parents were still at work and Tim was at a track meet, Laura suggested they sit on the front lawn, in full view of the entire neighborhood.

"Right," Ryan agreed. "All we need is for somebody to start stories about us being in your house alone, even if our parents hadn't said I wasn't to come over when they aren't home."

In a few blunt words, he explained his latest predicament. Laura listened without interrupting.

"I wish I could say my dad might hire you, but he can't use kids in his business at all."

"Yeah, my dad can't get me on at Lockwood Assembly either. Even my uncle doesn't have that much to do at his farm right now. I'd spend more time driving back and forth than I would working anyway."

Laura snapped her fingers. "Driving, that's it. You know that Pizza Paradise that just opened on Fletcher? About half a block from the Orpheum Theater."

Ryan furrowed his brows, trying to place it. "Oh, yeah, they had a coupon in the paper for a free pizza if you bought a large special."

"Right. They had a sign in the window advertising for drivers to deliver pizzas. I don't know what the hours or pay or age requirements are. It might be too late at night for you."

"It's worth a try. The only problem with pizza delivery is you're setting yourself up to be ripped off."

"Yeah, I know, but I don't think any of the businesses will deliver in the rough section of town anymore. Remember when somebody tried getting the city council to pass an ordinance forcing them to make deliveries?"

Ryan nodded. "There really hasn't been that much in the paper about robberies since then. I can always ask. Thanks for the tip. If everything goes okay, I'll be back tonight to help you with your trig."

The "driver wanted" sign still hung in the window when Ryan drove up. Ironically, the building had been a service station before it became a pizza parlor.

A bell tinkled when he opened the door. Six booths occupied the right side of the room while a long counter and ovens took up the left. A mural of gondolas spread across the back wall. Ryan glanced around, thinking the place was deserted, until a mountain of flesh rose behind the counter.

"Hi. I saw your sign. If you're still looking for drivers, I've got my own car, and I've never had a ticket."

The manager, a beefy bleached blonde who looked like her own best customer, looked Ryan over as if he were asking for a personal loan instead of a job. He wondered if he should have ordered a pizza first. Only he couldn't afford it.

"How old are you?" she asked at last.

"I was seventeen the end of March."

She stroked her double chins thoughtfully. "I'd prefer someone older but they lose interest when I tell them the hours. Friday and Saturday evenings, four to midnight. Minimum wage and you can keep the tips. If any."

The hours were terrible but given a choice of delivering pizzas or losing his car temporarily, he could sacrifice his weekends. He hoped Laura would understand. This job would certainly put an end to gossip about how he and Laura spent their Friday and Saturday nights.

"I'd like to give it a try. I have a VW Bug. Very economical on gas." He hoped he didn't have to pay for the gas himself.

"I have a couple white Camaros out back with our company logo on them. You'll drive one for all your deliveries. I'll give you a credit card for the gas, in case you have to fill it during the evening. Just make sure you give it back to me before you go home every night."

"Yes, ma'am." Ryan shifted his weight from one

foot to the other, not sure what he should say or do next. "Uh . . . I can give you a reference. Mr. Dennison has the service station over on Whitmore. I've worked for him since March. He had to let me go because his business has fallen off. I didn't get fired, or anything like that."

"Doesn't matter that much. By the way, I'm Mrs. Enzio. This is *my* business, not a franchise, and I expect to get my money's worth out of my employees. Do you know the city very well?"

"I know most of the streets in the northeast section." Ryan hoped that wasn't the wrong thing to say. Maybe he should have kept his mouth shut and gotten a city map.

"Don't worry about it. I've got some good maps. We don't deliver beyond four miles anyway, and no deliveries on the west end. I heard they don't like paying for their orders, and I'm not a charity."

"Uh . . . when would you like me to start?"

"This Friday." She scrutinized him carefully. "One more thing, you drive *alone*. No girlfriend or pals tagging along with you to help pass the long lonely hours."

"Oh, I wouldn't do that," Ryan hastily assured her.

"See that you don't." She looked him up and down again. "I suppose you'll be wanting the night off for your prom. When is it?"

Prom? Oh jeez, I forgot about the prom. "Third Saturday in May. I don't remember the exact date."

"One Saturday I can let you have off—for your girl's sake, not yours. She shouldn't have to miss the prom just because you're working."

"No, ma'am." Ryan knew he should feel grateful for her concern and generosity.

"Be here at three-thirty Friday. You can wear jeans if you want and I'll give you one of our company T-shirts. It has our logo on the front."

After a few more words on the business, Ryan exited through the back door so he could take a look at the car he'd be driving. The driver's door bore the inscription "Pizza Paradise" and a huge pizza adorned the hood. Not exactly his choice of a vehicle but then it was better than having to rack up miles on the Bug.

On the drive over to Laura's after supper, he started thinking about the prom. No matter how he added it up, he couldn't figure out a way to pay for his insurance, rent a tux, buy the tickets, flowers, pictures, and take Laura out for dinner.

Not unless some pizza lover gives me a hundred-dollar tip. He pulled to a stop in front of her house, still in a quandary about how to stretch his money. *I can't ask Dad. He couldn't have made that plainer if he'd written it on the bathroom mirror. Maybe I can find a second job after school or during the day on Saturdays.*

With heavy heart, he walked up the driveway to the door.

"I got the job but it's going to take my weekend evenings," he told Laura.

"I'm glad you found something. Tell me about it while I fix some Cokes, then we can go downstairs."

"You have to see Mrs. Enzio to believe her. I forgot to ask if there's a Mr. Enzio. Anyway, she made it clear that she's the boss and I take my orders from her."

"Does she run the place alone?"

"She said she has a girl come in to help in the shop, and there are two other drivers. She was all alone when I stopped in today."

Laura handed Ryan his Coke and led the way downstairs.

"I know what you're going through. I wish I could find a better job than working at the Knitting Basket on Saturdays, but nobody wants to hire kids and my parents won't let me work later than eight at night."

"Tell me about it," said Ryan despondently. "If you work during the day Saturday and I work in the evening, when are we ever going to see each other?"

Laura gave him a quick smile. "Sunday afternoons. Or is that a special time for your family?"

"We used to go to my grandma and grandpa's once a month but they're living in a retirement residence now so they come to visit us. Maybe another job will turn up and I can quit this one."

"I hope so. Until one does, we'll survive."

Ryan slid down on the couch so that his head rested on the edge of the top cushion. "I was afraid you might tell me to take a walk."

"You aren't getting rid of me that easily," she said, squeezing his hand. "I had to work too hard to get you."

"You did, huh? You've been taking pot shots at me for almost five years."

"Pot shots? I bring excitement, challenge and stimulating conversation into your life and you accuse me of taking pot shots!"

Ryan tossed a Kleenex at her. "You call it stimulating conversation when you tell the world the dodo bird isn't extinct, it willed its brain to Ryan Archer? And what about the time you said I had the personality of a bowl of overcooked spinach?"

"You said I had the personality of an abandoned toll booth."

"Overcooked spinach sounds worse. I'll bet you used to lie awake nights thinking up insults."

"I thought of the spinach when Mom served some one night. I don't think I could eat spinach and liver if I were starving to death."

"Or lima beans. My mother loves lima beans. I sure was glad when the price went up and she stopped cooking them so often." Ryan took a long swallow of Coke, as if to wash down the memory of lima beans.

Laura giggled. "We must be soul mates. We hate the same things. My aunt makes a casserole she calls tuna surprise. The surprise is that anybody can eat it without gagging. Tim and I think she should offer it to the Defense Department as a secret weapon. Three days of eating that stuff and any enemy would surrender."

"On that happy note, it's time to attack the trig assignment. Where's your book?"

The sound of feet above them, followed by Tim's appearance, was their only break for the next hour. He offered to share his plate of peanut-butter cookies.

Laura glanced at Ryan, raising her eyebrows. "How do you rate? The only thing he ever offers me is the empty plate to go get more."

"You're aren't a basketball player," said Ryan. "Tim knows what counts in life."

"You bet I do, and it isn't a sister who takes classes in how to talk more."

When the cookies were gone and he'd left, Ryan glanced at the banjo clock. "About time for me to leave, too. Were the cookies for real, or was that his way of checking up on us again?"

"Both. He's taking this smear campaign very seriously. Now he can truthfully tell his friends he was with us while we did our homework.''

Ryan sighed, slowly shaking his head. "If it makes your family feel better about me, okay, but I can't say I like being chaperoned by a kid.''

"It's one of the things we have to endure. You noticed I didn't greet him with open arms.''

"Yeah. By the way, Mrs. Enzio said I could have the night of the prom off. Is it okay for you to go?''

"Mom said she couldn't see any reason why we shouldn't, but she'd like it better if we double-dated. Do you think Matt might ask Sue?''

Ryan gave her an impulsive hug. "He's been practicing asking her for weeks, but he hasn't worked up the nerve to do it yet. Tell Sue to give him some encouragement.''

Since it was still daylight out, Laura kissed Ryan good night before they went upstairs. Still a very short kiss, by his former standards. If that's the way Laura wanted it, that's the way it would be.

At home, he sat down with pencil and paper and tried figuring out how much it would cost for the prom. The amount depressed him. Even if he wore his suit instead of renting a tux, it would still be cutting it close.

I can't take a girl in a formal to McDonald's for dinner. If nothing else, I can go back to mowing lawns.

The following morning, he talked with one of the college representatives who periodically visited the school. His PSAT score, National Honor Society, awards in the annual Science Fair, and the fact that he was vice-president of Physics Club made a good impression. The man extolled the college's science department, emphasizing that all professors had Ph.Ds.

The office secretary gave Ryan a late admittance slip for class. As he passed Laura's locker, he saw something written on it in blue marker pen. The message was basically the same as had been on the girls' room mirror.

Ryan promptly returned to the office and asked to see Mr. Sands, the assistant principal.

"What's the problem, Ryan?" asked the portly man, adjusting his glasses to take a closer look. "You seem upset about something."

"I am! Somebody's written a filthy message on Laura Nettleton's locker and I'd like a custodian to clean it off before she sees it. It's in blue marker, so they'll need some special cleanser."

Mr. Sands reached for his phone and punched out the three numbers for the head custodian. Instructions given, he turned back to Ryan. "Any idea who's behind this?"

"I wish I knew. I didn't break up with another girl to date Laura, so it isn't like a jealous girlfriend. At least, I don't think so."

"And that makes you all the more determined not to give in. What about Laura and an ex-boyfriend?"

Ryan tried not to let his face show how stupid he considered that suggestion. "The first time, it was lipstick on the mirror in the girls' room."

"Ah, yes, Mrs. Crawley mentioned something about that, but she didn't mention the girl's name."

"What worries me is they might spray paint something on the building next. You know how long it took to get off the stuff the seniors did last year."

Mr. Sands nodded. "Had to be sandblasted. You don't wash brick. Well, if that does happen, Mrs.

98

Crawley will turn it over to the police. She's still angry about the seniors, and if she ever gets a hint of who was involved, she'll have the school board bill the parents for the cost involved.''

Study hall was almost over by the time Ryan finally reported. He opened his history book and put his elbows on either side of it, then propped his chin on his upraised hands. From a distance, he looked like he was studying. While staring at the book, he pondered this latest incident. It was getting more public. What next, and how much could Laura stand before she decided he wasn't worth it?

''What's the special of the day?'' asked Ryan, joining Matt and Peter in the cafeteria line.

''Barf on a bun,'' said Matt. ''The alternative is oatmeal burgers, guaranteed to have seen real meat at least once on their way to the oven.''

''If the school board hadn't made this a closed campus, I'd go out for lunch,'' muttered Ryan.

''So would everybody else,'' said Peter. ''Then the government would go bankrupt because they couldn't sell all this surplus junk to the kids held prisoners in school cafeterias. We're doing our duty for our country.''

Ryan was close enough to see the lumpy, brownish mass a white-aproned cook was ladling onto an under-sized bun. ''You know, I think I just might go back to packing a lunch. At least you know what you're getting with a peanut-butter-and-jelly sandwich.''

When they'd gotten their meal and joined Jason and Craig, Ryan told them about Laura's locker.

''Does she know about it?'' asked Matt.

''I don't think so. And I'm not sure I should tell her. I just hope nobody else saw it.'' Ryan looked at his peas, a sickly yellowish green, and wondered which century they'd been cooked.

Peter, who'd opted for the oatmeal burger, then drowned it in ketchup, mustard, and pickles, took a big bite. Ketchup immediately squirted out the other side, running down his hands. He swore once and grabbed a napkin.

"If Laura does know about it, I don't think it will bother her all that much," he said. "She's tough enough to take anything."

"Laura isn't the iron woman everybody thinks she is," Ryan said, annoyed to find himself in a defensive position once more. "It's her way of protecting herself, just like a turtle's shell. She's a very sweet and sensitive girl, and this whole thing has upset her, whether it shows or not."

"Laura? Give me a break!" scoffed Jason.

Matt spoke up. "Why don't you give Laura a break? You don't even know her."

"Hey, I've been in classes with the Libber just as long as you have," Jason protested, "and I have never once seen that girl being sweet or sensitive. Sometimes she's nice or even funny, but sensitive? No way."

Ryan pushed his tray aside, a serious expression on his face. "Guys, Laura is my girl. You're my friends. I don't like hearing you knock her. It's hard enough to put up with the rest of this crap."

Peter regarded him intently, then sighed loudly. "Okay, we got the message, and I agree what's happening isn't fair. As long as I don't have to be around her self-righteous act, I guess I can stand her."

"So what's this job of yours like?" asked Craig.

"It's better than nothing but that's about all you can say for it."

"You get any free pizzas?" asked Jason.

"She didn't mention it. Considering the size of Mrs. Enzio, I think she's eats the leftovers."

They commiserated with him over the loss of his old job. "I was really counting on that dough for my car insurance," griped Ryan.

Peter gave him a sympathetic look. "I know the feeling. My insurance is on monthly premiums, not quarterly, and some months I really sweat it out, wondering if I'm going to make it. It wouldn't be so bad if bus boys got a share of the tips. Some places they do."

"Mrs. Enzio says I can keep my tips. I have a feeling they aren't going to be enough to help much."

When Ryan looked around the cafeteria for Laura after lunch, she'd already gone. Laura had explained that some days she liked to lunch with her friends for girl talk. Since Ryan felt the same way about his pals, he agreed. They had lunch together on alternate days. They also hoped it would squelch some of the gossip.

She was talking to Mrs. Kingsley when he and Matt arrived in English. Taking her seat, she turned to Matt with an impish smile.

"My brother has challenged you and Ryan to a basketball shoot-out. A fan of yours would like to watch it. Could you come over Saturday about one?"

Matt flushed, glancing hastily at Ryan. "I wish I could, but I'm working twelve to nine Saturdays."

"I thought you worked all day Saturdays," said Ryan to Laura.

"We'll be closed this weekend because Mrs. Overacker has to go to a funeral out of town. She

101

doesn't trust me to run the place alone.'' She turned back to Matt. "Would you have time before you go to work? Maybe a morning match?"

"I'm not sure. Ma usually has a lot of chores for me Saturday mornings. She works all week and that's the day we have to pitch in and help clean up the place."

"Sounds familiar," said Laura. "My mother only works mornings at Daddy's office but we get the same routine. How are you fixed for Sunday?"

"I think it would be okay. It's not my week to work."

"I'll see if Sue can make it and let you know."

"You're . . . uh . . . sure Sue *wants* to be there?"

Laura's grin and twinkling eyes seemed to reassure him. "She practically twisted my arm off trying to convince me she *had* to be there to cheer for you."

Ryan winked at Matt. "Be glad she's not a liberated woman threatening to scalp you if we don't win."

Ryan told Laura about her locker during their drive home. She glanced at him, a soft smile on her face.

"Thanks for telling me. Marcy had a pass to the library second hour and saw it. She told me when she came back, but it was gone by the time class was over. Thanks for taking care of it."

"Somebody may not like you, but Matt loves you. He was ten feet off the ground when he left school."

"Sue does have that effect on boys, and it's not just her fabulous figure. She flutters those big brown eyes and they fall at her feet. Sometimes I'm so envious, I'd like to strangle her. Why was I born with brains instead of sex appeal?''

"I think you're very sexy." Ryan grinned, then opened his door and stepped out of reach. "Just like that cactus."

Chapter 7

"How's it going?" asked Matt, walking into the Archer garage the next evening and bending down to peer at Ryan's engine.

"Sticky valve. Think I got it fixed. All I need is a major overhaul when I'm living on loose change." He straightened up, wiping his hands on a greasy rag, a little surprised to see Matt. "At least I won't have to use my car to make deliveries when I start that job tomorrow."

"Laura give you any hassles about your car?"

Ryan closed up the back, making sure it was latched. "She loves it; it's just her size. One of the first things she said to me was that I have the neatest car."

A broad grin split Matt's face. "So *that's* when you fell in love with her."

"Could be. Any girl with the good taste to like both me and my car has to be something special."

"Right. Uh . . . Sunday's okay to go over to Laura's."

Ryan glanced at his friend, observing the nervousness lurking beneath the surface. He put the grease rag and tools he'd been using back on the end shelf of the garage and led the way into the house.

"Want something to drink?" Ryan opened the refrigerator and examined the contents. "Root beer, Sprite, iced tea, cranapple, or milk."

"Sprite's fine."

After filling two glasses, the boys retreated to Ryan's room. Each took one end of the bed.

"I'll tell Laura we can make it. I guess Sue is spending the night with her."

"Oh." Matt took a sip of his pop. "I guess there isn't any reason to call about picking her up then. She lives only a few blocks from us," he hastily explained.

"She could probably use a ride home."

Matt brightened. "Yeah. Uh . . . what's the plan? We just shoot baskets with her brother and his pals?"

"Laura and Sue are fixing a barbecue supper for us. Oh, yeah, I was supposed to tell you about that. Sue's a home ec major and Laura says she's a fantastic cook."

"I can relate to good food," conceded Matt. He stared at the neatly lined bookshelf on the wall for several moments as if groping for a way to express himself. "Uh . . . is that it, shoot baskets and have a barbecue?"

Ryan bit back a smile, knowing exactly what his friend was going through, having so recently experienced the same uncertainties himself. If Matt couldn't brighten up his conversation with something more than "uh," Sue might not be terribly impressed.

"I'm sure Laura will plan a time for us to be alone with the girls. Just don't expect too much; her family is still around whenever I go to visit. I don't know if they'll check up on us quite as often with a double date."

"You asked her about Sue and me?"

"Not exactly. I sort of hinted you were interested in Sue, and she said when they had that pajama party that Sue asked her to ask me if I could find out if you liked her."

"Oh."

"Sue thinks that mustache is very sexy."

"Yeah?" Matt touched it gingerly. He still looked as if he were walking barefoot through broken glass. "Uh . . . how did you get through that first date with Laura?"

"It was pretty tense for a while. Believe it or not, I think Laura was more nervous than I was. It helps that she has a sense of humor. Until her brother showed up—she was ready to kill him."

"Yeah, my brother never wanted me around when he was with a girl."

"After this smear campaign started, Laura calmed down a little. She still doesn't like having her brother around, but she's afraid if she yells too loud about it, her parents won't let me come over at all."

Matt gave Ryan a worried look. "You mean those kids are going to be around the whole time? Even after the game?"

"No, Laura said they'll all go home when it's over. After we eat, she said we could either play one of their board games or watch a movie." Ryan grinned slowly. "She's hoping you'll relax enough to ask Sue to the prom, and so is Sue. Sue definitely won't ask you."

Matt flushed. He tried to cover his embarrassment by finishing off his drink. "I'd like to go with her. I started to ask her twice when I was walking her to her locker after psych, but I just couldn't say it. Guess I was too scared she'd say no. Or already had a date."

106

"Well, she doesn't, so now you can ask her. They're already planning on a double date. *That* was Mrs. Nettleton's idea. She thinks there's safety in numbers."

"A double date's okay," said Matt, nodding. "With you and Laura around, maybe I'll actually be able to talk to Sue without sounding like a moron."

Ryan, seeing Cheryl passing in the hall, got up and closed his door. He didn't want her butting in. He then turned on his stereo to make sure she couldn't hear anything by listening at the door.

"One nice thing about Sue, you'll never have to worry about her taking any shots at you. She doesn't regard men as the 'enemy' the way Laura does. I know it's mostly an act, but still, Laura does intimidate most guys."

"You know, I think Laura's really a little afraid of boys because she's so small, and she puts on this big liberated act to keep them at a distance. The best defense is a good offense stuff. Like Peter. He wouldn't touch her on a bet."

Ryan thought about that for a moment. "I know what you mean, but I think there's more to it than that with Peter. Somewhere along the line she must have really burned him. Jason and Craig might gripe about her but they came and sat at her table after the smear campaign started."

"You could have a point there," agreed Matt, nodding. "Peter doesn't have much of a sense of humor and if Laura shot him down in a class the way she does you, he couldn't think fast enough to come back with a snappy answer."

"When it comes to a duel of wits with Laura, you'd better be *en garde* full time. And I've got the scars to prove it."

"Hey, listening to you two was the only thing that saved an entire class from dying of boredom when we took that required semester of geography that lasted about fifty years. As for scars, you've left a few yourself."

"Yeah, I have to admit it's been a fair fight. I kind of miss it now." Ryan looked at Matt, his voice earnest. "You know how a dill pickle always adds something to a hamburger and how flavorless it tastes without one? The dill pickle has gone out of our duels."

Matt fell back on the bed and roared. "If Laura ever found out you called her a dill pickle, she'd have your hide."

"She'd take it as a compliment," said Ryan, grinning. "Sue's more like a chocolate-coated marshmallow."

"Funny how she and Laura are friends, isn't it? Sue is so feminine with those long eyelashes and fluttery eyes, and Laura's the super-competent, liberated woman."

"Not at home, she isn't. But she's never going to be like Sue, and I'm not sure I'd want her to. I've gotten too used to arguing with her."

Matt glanced at his watch. "I'd better be going. I have to pick up some stuff at the store on the way home. Ma said if I want to take my lunch, I have to fix it."

"Think I'll do the same."

Ryan walked out to Matt's car with him. Just before leaving, Matt popped his head out the window. "What should we wear? On Sunday."

"You'll need your tennis shoes, shorts, and T-shirt for the game. Laura said we could change afterward. The girls are planning to wear jeans for the barbecue."

                    *   *   *

Friday morning, Shelly, one of the worst gossips in school, found pages torn from an anonymous diary in the locker room. No real names appeared on the pages, only frequent references to Lover Boy and his sexual prowess.

Ryan heard about it twenty minutes before Laura did. She dismissed it when Ryan tried apologizing during lunch. Just before they finished, Shelly sauntered up to their table.

"Somebody really likes the way your boyfriend does his stuff. I'll bet you didn't know he was that good."

Laura glanced at the pages thrust under her nose, then looked her tormentor straight in the eyes. "Congratulations, you've learned how to write. Is this your first manuscript for the porno magazines? And you didn't even write it with crayons."

"I didn't write this crap!" She said it loud enough to be heard all over the cafeteria.

"Not that literate, huh? Did you have to get somebody to read it to you, too?"

"Up yours," snarled Shelly, unaware of Mrs. Crawley bearing down on her. The principal silently relieved Shelly of her papers.

"Go wait in my office, Shelly." Mrs. Crawley glanced over the pages while Ryan wished he could evaporate. Laura calmly finished her lunch. "More of the same trash. Any idea who's responsible, Ryan? Does the handwriting look familiar?"

Ryan peered at it, relieved to find that he didn't recognize it. "No, ma'am."

"In that case, I'll just have to ask teachers for samples of the handwriting of their students. Maybe we can find our anonymous author. I'm afraid the person may eventually try painting these messages, and I will *not* have a repetition of that!''

Mrs. Crawley kept the papers as evidence, determined to hand them over to the police and a handwriting expert if the slightest dab of paint appeared anywhere in the building. Once word of that got around, nobody seemed to think harassing Laura and Ryan was that much fun any more. Not if it might mean a trip to the principal's office—or the police station.

''I think that diary might have been the last of it,'' Laura told Ryan on the way home. ''Mrs. Crawley doesn't care that much about what it said, but she's determined to protect her building to the bitter end.''

Ryan, in line behind a slow moving garbage truck, agreed. ''You know, I think the only reason Crawley makes such a big issue about the building is because she can't really do much about some of the bigger problems, like drugs, drinking parties, or the pregnant girls who keep dropping out.''

''I hadn't thought of that. You could be right. If it puts a stop to the smear campaign, I don't care what her motives are.''

Sunday afternoon, a small kink—in the form of a younger sister—appeared in Ryan's plans. Cheryl announced she was going along to the game and barbecue as Tim's guest. Ryan informed her she had to stay home. Cheryl insisted Tim had as much right to ask a girl to visit him as Laura had to ask a boy to visit her.

Mayhem, mutilation, and possible murder seemed imminent when Laura called the Archer home and asked to speak to Cheryl. Cheryl answered with a smirk that nearly cost her a broken neck. She cradled the phone close to her, doing her best to keep Ryan from hearing any of the conversation. After a brief discussion, she triumphantly handed it to her furious brother.

"Laura wishes to speak to you." Cheryl dodged out of reach and stuck out her tongue.

Ryan made a superhuman effort to calm his temper before greeting Laura.

"Hi, Ryan. *Somebody,* who will feature prominently in the obituary column tomorrow, just told us that he invited all his friends to stay for the barbecue. Mother thought it was a great idea."

"You're kidding," said Ryan dolefully.

"I wish I were! I knew the kids were coming for the game, but he didn't mention the barbecue until ten minutes ago. Dad is on the way to the store to buy more food. I'd like to barbecue my brother!"

Ryan groaned. "I don't even want to think about telling Matt. He's been counting the seconds."

"You should see Sue. She's ready to take Tim apart with her bare hands, and Sue is the easiest-to-get-along-with-person I've ever known."

Ryan pulled out one of the kitchen chairs to sit down. Cheryl had had sense enough to retreat to her room. Ryan considered the possibility of locking her in.

"Isn't there a slave trader somewhere that we could sell them to?" He wasn't entirely joking when he asked.

"Ryan, I've never been so mad at my brother in my life," said Laura, sounding on the verge of tears. "Mom just keeps saying how wonderful it is that we're finally getting along better."

"Maybe they're still trying to protect your reputation. You know what your mother said about safety in numbers.''

''That's not the point. I could accept the basketball game and the girls coming to watch, but when Mom let them horn in on our party, that was too much! Sue and Matt are so shy they'll be miserable with all those kids around.''

''Hey, it's okay. I'm not crazy about the idea, but we're stuck with it. We'll just have to roll with the punches. See you in a few minutes.''

Ryan replaced the receiver and yelled to Cheryl, his anger still very plain. She stayed at the kitchen door, out of his reach. He noticed that she'd changed to her new acid-washed jeans and teddy bear sweatshirt.

''You may be my sister but you're not my idea of a double date. Don't you *ever* pull anything like this again.''

''Tim *asked* me,'' said Cheryl defiantly.

''Laura isn't very happy with him, either. Wait here while I get the rest of my gear.''

In his room, he relieved some of his hostility by punching his pillow several times. He suspected it was Cheryl's idea to crash the barbeque, but Tim was probably eager to keep an eye on things, especially if he had read that ''diary.''

He sighed, defeated. *When you go with a nice girl, you get concerned parents—and kid brothers. By the time they trust me with Laura, we'll be ready for an old-age pension.*

Jeans, socks and a windowpane plaid shirt went into his gym bag, along with a towel and deodorant. Nice of Laura's mother to tell the guys they could shower after the game.

He ran a comb through his hair, pulled down his T-shirt, and grabbed the bag. As he passed through

112

the kitchen to the garage, Cheryl fell in step behind him.

"Get in the car and keep your mouth shut."

They made the trip to Nettletons' in ominous silence. Matt pulled up while they were getting out of the car. Matt stared at Cheryl as if she were some strange apparition.

"You're not baby-sitting, are you?" he asked irritably.

Ryan tersely filled him in. Cheryl's defiance withered under Matt's icy stare. All three silently walked toward the house. Laura and Sue met them at the door, looking a little glum.

"Come in," said Laura, with a forced smile.

She introduced Cheryl and Matt to her parents, then led the way to the family room where Tim, three girls, and two boys were already watching a Disney cartoon on the VCR.

"Just what I wanted to do on my day off," mumbled Matt under his breath. Ryan nudged him in the ribs.

"We can start the game as soon as the other guy gets here," said Tim nervously from his position on the floor.

"No hurry," said Ryan.

Cheryl tentatively perched on the end of the couch with the other girls. Ryan and Matt leaned against the wall, arms folded across their chests. Sue looked at the ground and made no move to talk to the guys. Laura politely asked each of her guests what they'd like to drink. Time dragged by. Laura returned with a tray and Sue helped her pass out the drinks.

"Okay, everybody, let's hold it," said Ryan, breaking the silence. "I think the younger generation has figured out that joining a party without telling the older generation was not a smart idea. Instead of sitting around sulking, I think the time has come to work out a compromise.''

''What kind of compromise?'' Tim's voice ended in a high squeak that obviously embarrassed him.

''Our team is going to take on your team. It's a foregone conclusion that we'll cream you so we'll spot you twenty-five points.''

Tim's group objected in unison. One pointed out that they outnumbered the older boys, even if they were shorter. Ryan held out his hands for quiet.

''The stakes. We play for one hour. At the end of that time, the winners get one hour of watching a movie down here *alone* while the losers take a hike. We meet back here at—'' He turned to Laura. ''What time is dinner?''

''Five.''

''Meet at four-thirty so everybody can help get the stuff ready.''

Tim got up off the floor, a bit of a swagger in his stance. ''We are gonna smear you guys so bad you won't know what hit you.''

''Yeah?'' said Matt. ''We're gonna beat you so bad you'll barbecue your basketball.''

Tim led his group out through the garage, whooping wildly. Laura gazed at Ryan, eyebrows raised.

''Nice move. Do you think it will work?''

Ryan grinned. ''Can't miss. If they win, they come down here and we play a board game on your picnic table. If we win, they stay outside and play another game or chase themselves.''

''I cannot *believe* my mother letting Tim get away with this,'' Laura sputtered. Her blue eyes sparked angrily.

"She did, so let's get on with Plan B. The day may not turn out to be a total disaster."

Matt sighed. "Let's go whip the pants off those guys. I'm playing for real now."

Ryan and Matt were three inches taller than the tallest of Tim's team. Mr. Nettleton was drafted to referee, and Laura's mother, pleased to see her family together, served as scorekeeper. Tim's girls took the east side of the driveway, Laura and Sue the lawn on the west.

The younger girls had obviously gotten together to decide on a "uniform" for the day. Each of them wore a teddy bear sweatshirt with jeans. Laura and Sue wore cotton sweaters. Though Laura looked nice in hers, she didn't fill it with quite the distracting curves Sue had. Ryan winked at them, then lined up with Tim for the flip to decide who got the first ball.

Ryan and Matt had five baskets the first three minutes, even when Tim's team tried playing three on one. The girls screamed and cheered; Cheryl even offered to join in the game. Tim brusquely told her it was a man's game. Before long, people were coming from all over the neighborhood to watch.

When the score reached 57–21, Ryan suggested they split the teams and start over.

"We'll split alphabetically," said Ryan. "Archer, Hopkins, and Knopf against Maddox, Nettleton, and VanderLahr. Okay, men, that is the enemy. What do we do with the enemy?"

"Kill 'em!" yelled his teammates.

"Are we going to let those bums make us look bad in front of our cheerleaders?" asked Matt. "We gotta wipe 'em out, men."

Mr. Archer blew his whistle and the game started again in earnest. Since Ryan and Matt had been playing together for so many years, each knew all the other's moves. The game went fast and furious, the score staying neck and neck.

Cheryl practically screamed herself hoarse cheering Tim on. He was so excited when he scored two baskets in a row that he ran over and hugged her.

Ryan caught a glimpse of a couple of the older men making a bet on the game. Glancing around, he was even more surprised to see eighty-six-year-old Mr. Underhill watching in his wheelchair. His granddaughter had brought him over.

When the score tied at 47–47, Mr. Nettleton blew his whistle and declared the game a draw.

"Overtime," yelled Tim.

"The game is over. Your mother and the girls have to fix supper. Tim, show the boys where to shower. Two minutes each."

One of the men who'd bet on the game came over to Ryan. "Are you boys playing again next week?"

"Maybe later this summer," said Ryan.

Laura and Ryan brought up the rear when the rest of the kids entered the house. Laura stopped him in the garage.

"Tim says it started when Cheryl told him she didn't believe any of those things that were written about us. He swears he doesn't remember how they got around to today's game or the barbecue. He asked her before he even thought about it."

"I'll bet!"

"He's just started noticing girls—and it would be her."

"I don't think he noticed her at all," said Ryan, annoyed that his suspicions had been confirmed. "She went after him. She keeps trying to pretend she's

116

sixteen instead of fourteen, and I think this was her way of getting Mom to let her have a boyfriend."

Laura gave him a puzzled look. "I don't quite follow you."

"She'll tell Mom that we're going together so it should be okay for her to go with Tim, sort of all in the family."

"Sneaky. I'd never think of anything like that."

Ryan laughed and kissed her. "No, you wouldn't, but then boys aren't the center of your universe."

"One is now." Laura hugged him quickly, before joining the other kids in the family room.

Ryan looked around for Tim. "You owe me one," he said, looking directly into the younger boy's eyes. "Don't let Cheryl talk you into any more crazy ideas."

Tim gulped and nodded guiltily. Ryan felt a little sorry for the kid, catching it from Laura and Sue, and now from him. He probably hadn't realized what he was getting into, but then he hadn't had years of living with Cheryl's sneaky ways.

"I guess I'll check with Laura first next time. She said I should have told her sooner."

"That would be a very smart idea," agreed Ryan.

By the time the boys had taken turns showering, Mr. Nettleton had the charcoal burning. Sue carefully dipped chicken in her own special barbecue sauce and arranged the pieces on the grill. Laura put Cheryl and the other girls to work preparing the outside tables while she finished the fruit salad.

"Won't it take a long time for that chicken to cook?" asked Ryan, joining Laura in the kitchen.

"Not too long. We partially cooked it in the microwave when we found out how many people we'd have."

"The day hasn't turned out to be so bad after all." Ryan sat down on a chair, out of Laura's way. "Anything I can help you with?"

"Peel and slice the bananas. As for today, Timothy is still living on borrowed time."

"I think he learned his lesson. He couldn't have been comfortable with all that tension when we first got here."

Laura glanced out the window and smiled. "Matt is helping Sue or maybe I should say, *trying* to help her."

Ryan chuckled. "Right now he's so happy, he wouldn't care if he barbecued his fingers. He's been practicing how to ask her to the prom."

"Do boys really worry about dating a girl for the first time?" She quickly sliced a piece of apple and reached for another piece.

Ryan gave her an incredulous look. "Yeah, they do! You think it's easy to pick up a phone and call a girl when you're not sure if she'll say yes?"

"I've never thought about it at all. You and Matt always seem so sure of yourselves that I figured you're too cool to worry."

"Laura, do you know how much sleep I lost trying to figure out if you liked me? And after what you said about my reputation, I didn't think you'd ever go out with me. Then I had to get through our first date."

Laura put the last of the apples into the bowl and declared her salad finished. She washed her hands, then took the chair beside Ryan, gazing intently into his eyes.

"Were you nervous because it was me or would you have felt that way with any girl?"

"Mostly because it was you. Other girls give me *some* encouragement before I ask them out."

She flushed, lowering her eyes. "I was afraid to encourage you. I didn't think you could ever possibly like me. Before we read the play, I mean."

"Weren't you nervous at all when you asked me to come over?"

"Yes. I rehearsed my speech several times the night before. I did have the advantage of knowing you were too much of a gentleman to refuse me in front of everyone. Even if you really didn't want to, you'd have said yes, then called me later to break the date."

"What would you have done if I'd said no?"

Laura gave him a smile that was full of feminine certainty. "I knew you wouldn't. Not after the way you kissed my hand. If you'd meant it as a joke, you'd have dropped it right away."

Ryan blinked. "Then why did you get so mad?"

"Because you didn't know you liked me yet. I could see the surprise in your eyes. And I was angry that you'd do something that personal in front of all those people. You didn't give me a fair chance to respond to you."

He was still having trouble absorbing all this. "When did you decide you liked me?"

"That day last fall when I was rushing into school in the morning with my arms loaded and my skirt caught in the door. Remember how my skirt pulled up?" Ryan nodded. "Peter made some dumb remark about seeing better legs on pigeons and you told him to shut up, then you opened the door and brushed my skirt down."

This informative conversation might have continued indefinitely if Laura's father hadn't entered the kitchen.

"Where's your mother?" he asked.

"Lying down. All the screaming gave her a headache."

After Mr. Nettleton walked down the hall, Laura whispered, "Before going to her room, Mom said she didn't think it was such a good idea to have so many kids here at once after all. We don't have this many when the pool's full."

"Good! I hope we've had our first and last—what is it—sextuple date."

"So do I! The junior generation is downstairs watching a tape of the Muppets, Matt and Sue are alone with the barbecue, and someday we may actually get to go out on a date. Life is looking up."

When Sue declared the chicken done, Laura started a human chain out the door to the picnic table. Mrs. Nettleton recovered long enough to join them for dinner, then returned to her room.

Laura and Sue headed the clean-up in the kitchen while Ryan and Matt supervised the boys in clearing up everything in the yard. Tim's group drifted off shortly afterward, except for Cheryl.

"I'd be happy to take you home," Matt told Sue.

"Thank you. Um . . . maybe we could all meet at my house next week. My sisters are both married so we won't have to worry about any more surprise guests."

Sue, who'd managed to carry her overnight bag with one hand when she arrived, now willingly surrendered it to Matt.

"The pest and I had better be going, too." After kissing Laura good night in the kitchen, Ryan called to Cheryl.

"I'm sorry it didn't turn out better," Laura said. "At least it got Sue and Matt together."

"I think maybe our siblings have something going, too."

On the way home, Cheryl happily confessed that she liked Tim and that he seemed to reciprocate her feelings.

"Great. After this, you like him on *your* time, not mine."

"Yes, Ryan," she said meekly.

Chapter 8

"Did you hear what happened in Mrs. Voronski's class today?" asked Laura. She and Ryan sat at her kitchen table, doing their latest English study guide together. "Some boy threw her big ivy out the window. Mrs. Voronski passed out paper and told everybody to write down what, if anything, they saw."

"And they all said Santa Claus or the Tooth Fairy did it. Like last fall when that nut was slashing the teachers' tires." Ryan knew only too well how fruitless most "official" school investigations were.

"A few wrote that," conceded Laura, "but remember, they caught the Mad Slasher finally. Anyway, four different people told who it was. When Mrs. Crawley called the boy in, he admitted it. He was mad because Mrs. Voronski sent home a poor work notice and his parents grounded him."

"I'm glad he didn't get away with it. But what's that got to do with us?"

Laura sighed softly, as if wondering how he could be so dense. "If a few people are willing to report something like that, it's possible we may find out who's behind all this garbage about us. If it keeps up, sooner or later somebody is going to see the person, and we'll either hear it directly or through the grapevine.''

Ryan nodded. "It's possible. I thought it was Therese at first, but she doesn't have any real reason. We were never going steady, and she was busy the last few times I asked her out.''

"Therese has never liked me very much. I've beaten her out too many times, starting back in second grade when I got to be room representative. I got the prize for selling the most Girl Scout cookies in our troop in sixth grade, and I was elected ninth grade secretary. She hasn't run against me for anything since.''

Ryan thought that over. "You've been the target of most of this stuff. Maybe she is out to get you. She sure doesn't care enough about me to be jealous.''

"Just proves she has neither taste nor intelligence,'' said Laura, slipping her arm around him for a quick hug.

"It sure took you long enough to develop taste and intelligence. I've been telling you for years that I'm gifted, charming, talented, and totally lovable,'' said Ryan, with an answering grin. He shifted in the chair, trying to find more leg room.

"And modest. Wait a minute,'' said Laura, rising. "I'll pull out the chairs on the other side of the table so you can stretch your legs.''

"That's the thing I hate most about going to the movies; they never have enough leg room. I guess they think all their customers are your size.''

"Leg room is no problem, it's trying to see. No matter where I sit, the person in front of me is always at least eight feet tall.''

"I guess we're doomed to spend the rest of our

lives watching movies on your VCR, even after your parents do approve of me.''

''Now that she's gotten to know you, Mom has decided those Lover Boy stories were exaggerated. Knowing your mother helped. I guess they had coffee together after they went to their first Weight Watchers meeting.''

''Yeah, Mom said talking about us got their minds off their diet problems. She never has liked that Lover Boy tag, and Dad doesn't dare laugh about it now.'' He gave Laura a meaningful look. ''You can stop stalling; the trig assignment isn't going to go away. What is it you need explained?''

Laura groaned. ''Everything except the page number. *That* number I understand.''

Friday morning's drizzle developed into a downpour by the time Ryan reported for work. Mrs. Enzio handed him the first orders and the money bag with ten dollars change.

''As slow as it's been today, this may be the only run you make all night,'' she said. ''I told Larry not to bother coming in tonight. Avoid Harrison Street; it's flooded.''

By the time Ryan returned, his jeans were soaked from the knees down and his shoes squished when he walked. The appreciation shown by his customers reached a grand total of one dollar and twenty-seven cents.

''I used up more gas than that,'' he muttered, slogging through the mud puddles to the restaurant.

''I thought you'd never get back,'' complained Mrs. Enzio crossly. ''A big party on Monterey ordered five large deluxe specials. That's over sixty bucks, so make sure you see the color of their money before you hand over so much as one olive."

Ryan maneuvered the boxes into the back of the car and arranged them so they wouldn't fall over. Something about the Monterey address seemed vaguely familiar, but he couldn't place it. Maybe one of the guys on the basketball team lived out that way.

Jeff Yarbrough lived there. The minute Ryan saw the Fiero in the driveway, he knew he'd have trouble. He rang the bell, knocked on the door, and finally banged on it, trying to be heard above the noise of the stereo.

"Why don't the neighbors call the cops?" he muttered. "They sure would in our neighborhood."

Therese opened the door. She held a can of beer in her hand and her eyes looked bloodshot. The buttons on her blouse had been done up wrong, making it lopsided. A malicious smile crossed her face.

"Do you have an invitation?"

"No, I have five pizzas and instructions to get the money before I deliver them."

Therese closed the door in his face and yelled for Jeff. Jeff jerked the door open and leered at Ryan. "Hi, Pizza Pete. Where's your pie?"

"Where's your money?" asked Ryan frostily.

"How much is it?" Jeff groped for his wallet.

"Sixty-four eighteen, with tax."

Jeff pulled out a handful of bills and started counting them. "Tough luck. I only got fifty-two."

"Then you only get four pizzas," said Ryan, taking the money before Jeff could argue.

He swiftly crossed the lawn, took four pizzas from the back and returned to the porch. Jeff almost dropped them grabbing them from Ryan. Ryan turned just in time to see the car door open as Therese grabbed the remaining pizza. She ran to the back of the house before Ryan could catch her.

Furious, Ryan returned to the front door and banged on it again. They ignored him. He opened it and walked in. A pair of sullen and hostile faces stared at him.

"Get out of my house," ordered Jeff.

"Just as soon as I get one pizza or twelve-fifty."

"Get out or I'll throw you out."

Ryan walked back to the door and held it open, careful to stay on the porch side. "Pay me or return the pizza."

"What if I don't? What are you gonna do about it?" asked Jeff in a menacing tone. "Report me to your boss? I'm scared, Archer, I'm really scared."

"All I want is the money or the pizza."

"You aren't gonna get either one. All you're gonna get is lost." Jeff shoved Ryan backward, knocking him off the porch. "You aren't gonna narc on us, either, Archer, 'cause if you do, I'll smash that beat-up old Bug you're so proud of. You just go back to work and say you *lost* the money."

Ryan slowly picked himself up. A cold rage, colder than his sodden clothes, filled him. "If I see so much as one scratch on my car, I know a Fiero that's going to have some scratches. Now give me the money."

Jeff shouted an obscenity and slammed the door. Ryan wearily returned to the car, trying to decide what to do next. If he returned short of the money, Mrs. Enzio might fire him and deduct the amount from his check. If he reported Jeff to the police, he'd be labeled a narc. The only thing he could do was pay for the pizza himself. But he only had three dollars until he got paid tomorrow.

I can't borrow from Matt. He took Sue out tonight. Maybe one of the other guys.

He drove to the nearest service station and used the pay phone to call Jason, Craig, and Peter. None was home.

If I ask Mom for the money, she'll want to know why, then she'll call the cops. Laura's the only one left.

Ryan slowly punched out Laura's number, his stomach a leaden lump. "Laura? I've got a problem. Could I stop by your place right away?"

"Certainly, Ryan. What's wrong?"

"I'll tell you when I get there. I'll come to the back door; I'm soaked."

He'd been in and out of the car so many times that the seat was now as wet as he was. *What will Laura say? No, what will she think? That I haven't got the guts to do the right thing. She isn't the one who has to make the decision.*

Feeling guilty and ashamed, he stopped at the curb and walked around to the back entrance where Laura waited for him. She pulled him inside in spite of his protests.

"Some kids from school ordered five pizzas and only paid for four. I left one in the car, and while I took the others to the door, they swiped it. If I come back short of the money I'll lose my job. None of the guys is home to help me out. If I narc I'll never live it down. Can I borrow nine dollars until tomorrow?"

Laura didn't bat an eye. "I'll get my purse." She returned in a moment and handed him a ten. "I don't have any change."

Ryan took it, feeling worse than ever. "I can't turn them in, Laura."

"Ryan, believe it or not, I do understand. Know-

127

ing some of the kids in our school, I'd guess that they were drinking and they think this is all a big joke—buy four pizzas and steal one.''

He looked at her and swallowed, feeling a little better about himself. "That's about the size of it. Ticked off as I am, I don't want to make trouble.''

"It isn't robbery, you know, it's blackmail. They're enjoying the big joke. And they just might repeat it, as long as they get away with it.'' She bit her lip, lowering her eyes, then looking at him again. "Sorry, didn't mean to preach.''

Ryan thought about that all the way back to Pizza Paradise. They did enjoy it. They'd probably invite half the senior class over to eat those pizzas and laugh about the fool they'd made of him. When word got around that Ryan Archer would pay for the pizzas himself rather than be called a narc, more kids would rob him. Before long he'd be working for nothing while those jerks ate up his paycheck.

"And I thought all I had to worry about was how to pay for my insurance and the prom. I just hope Mrs. Enzio doesn't fire me,'' he muttered to himself as he pulled up behind Pizza Paradise.

Sitting in the car, watching the rain beat against the windshield, Ryan rehearsed several different ways he could tell Mrs. Enzio what had happened.

"Oh, to hell with it. I'll just tell her the plain facts.''

He climbed out of the car, grabbed the money bag, and dashed to the door just as a huge lightning bolt lit up the sky. The way his luck was going tonight, he wouldn't be surprised if it hit him.

"They paid for four pizzas and stole the other one out of the car when I went to the door,'' said Ryan, counting out the money to his employer.

"They did, huh?"

The way she was staring at him, Ryan wasn't sure she believed him. He cleared his throat nervously. The aroma of pepperoni drifted to his nostrils, bringing a sudden burst of saliva. Jeez, one minute his throat was dry, the next he felt like he was going to drown. He swallowed.

"I've got enough to pay for it myself. I mean, it was my responsibility to collect the money."

"I don't set my drivers up to get robbed and I'm not going to let anybody think I do. You're not the first kid who's had to face this kind of crap."

She reached for the tab with the order, glancing at the phone number. Her pudgy fingers punched out the number with the force of a heavyweight contender. Watching her, Ryan thought she could probably take on the world heavyweight champ with one hand tied behind her. He reminded himself that his employer was not a lady to mess around with.

"This is the owner of Pizza Paradise," she barked into the phone. "You've got exactly ten minutes to be here with twenty-five bucks in cash or the police will be visiting you in eleven minutes."

She slammed down the receiver and smiled, quite pleased with herself. "You deserve a tip when you have to work that hard to make a delivery."

"Do you think it will work?" asked Ryan uncertainly.

"You bet your sweet life it will! Nobody rips off my drivers. You let scum get away with something like that once, and before you know it, I'll be out of business. I'm not running a free lunch counter. If anybody's going to eat my profits, it's *me!*"

Ryan looked at the giant menu on the wall, then back at Mrs. Enzio. He wouldn't touch a straight line like that for a lifetime supply of pizzas. Keeping his face straight required concerted effort.

"Um . . . any more deliveries for me to make?"

"Naw, I think I'll close up after those bums get here. I'm too old to work this hard for this little."

Jeff Yarbrough sheepishly slunk through the door eight minutes later, cash in hand. He looked pale and very worried. Mrs. Enzio stalked around the counter, grabbed the money with one hand and the front of his shirt with the other. Jeff might be taller, but she outweighed him by at least a hundred pounds. Jeff looked as if he'd just been declared the main course for a hungry lion.

"Listen, buster, I don't like the games you play. I am going to circulate your name, address, and phone number to every pizza joint in this town, telling them what kind of a deadbeat you are. Then I am going to have my attorney send a formal letter of complaint to your dear old daddy. Now get out of my place and don't ever come back!"

Jeff all but crawled out the door.

"And you tell that mealy-faced girlfriend of yours she's blacklisted, too," she yelled after him.

Ryan's mouth dropped open in pure surprise. At no time had he mentioned Therese.

"What was her name?" snapped Mrs. Enzio when Jeff had closed the door.

"Therese Deauville, but how did you—"

"She's hiding in the car. She didn't have the guts to come in here with him. Don't worry, I'll let her think I recognized her."

Ryan shifted uncomfortably, then stuffed his hands in his pockets for lack of something better to do. "Are you really going to blacklist them?"

"You bet I am, and I'm sending a copy of the

130

letter to his folks. It's like bad checks, you know? It won't take long for the word to get around. Other kids will think twice before they pull a stunt like this." She squinted at Ryan, as if expecting his support.

"They'll sure think about it if they know they're going to be circulated like a wanted poster."

"If more people stomped on these kids the first time they tried to pull a fast one, there'd be fewer criminals in the world. You let 'em get away with it and they try something bigger the next time and pretty soon it's grand larceny or murder. You gotta nip it in the bud."

Ryan started laughing. "I'll bring my girl down here to meet you some night. She'd like you."

"What's so funny about that?"

"Up to now, I thought she was the most independent woman in the world."

"I got news for you, kid, there were independent women long before somebody thought up women's lib, only they were called widows or deserted wives. They were left to run the farm or the business and raise the kids alone, and nobody ever gave them one damned bit of credit for having the guts or gumption to do it."

She banged open the cash register and put the five in, hesitated a moment, then handed Ryan the twenty. "You earned it. I imagine they were friends of yours, and you had the backbone to report them. Most kids would have paid for the pizza themselves without saying a word."

Ryan turned a dull red. "I was going to. Then I started thinking, why should I work for nothing just so they could make me look like an idiot."

"Your head's screwed on right. Now you get on

home and out of those wet clothes before you catch your death of pneumonia."

He grinned broadly, returning the twenty to her. "Could I order a large pepperoni first? I'd like to take it over to my girl's house."

She nodded brusquely, setting her chins in motion. "Pick it up in half an hour. That'll give you time to go home and change."

When he parked in the Nettleton driveway this time, his heart was considerably lighter. Even the rain had dwindled to a drizzle. Grabbing the pizza box, he headed for the door, salivating once more as the aroma filled his nostrils.

Laura met him, surprised, especially when she saw the pizza. "You stole it back?"

"It's a long story. Can we take this into the kitchen, then I'll give you all the gory details."

"I don't believe this," said Laura, when Ryan finished his story. "She actually grabbed Jeff by the shirt?"

"She sure did. Poor Jeff looked like he wished he'd never been born. She's built like a sumo wrestler."

They sat at the kitchen table eating half the pizza. Cheryl and Tim devoured the other half down in the family room. Laura's parents declined a share of the loot.

"And she's really going to circulate their names?"

"When I went back to pick up the pizza, she said she was sending a letter to Mrs. Crawley, too. I wouldn't be surprised to see her paint their names on a billboard. And not with lipstick."

Laura licked a bit of tomato paste off her thumb. Mrs. Enzio knew how to make a mean pizza. Laura promised herself she'd tell all her friends to give Pizza Paradise a try.

"What do you think Jeff's parents will do?"

Ryan shrugged. "I don't know. He's the only boy in a family of three girls and the apple of his father's eye. His father might threaten to sue Mrs. Enzio for defamation of character, or something like that."

"Maybe you'd better warn her."

"I already did. She said if he tries taking her into court, she'll ask why they weren't home to supervise the activities of their underage son." Ryan polished off the last of his slice, then washed it down with Coke. He felt content as well as full.

"Now *that* is a woman with the courage of her convictions," said Laura admiringly.

"I knew you'd like her." Ryan grinned. "Oh, before I forget." He returned her ten. "Thanks for bailing me out."

"You forgot the interest," said Laura, stretching up to kiss him.

"You taste like pepperoni," murmured Ryan, touching her lips again. "I've always been crazy about pepperoni."

Things went a lot better at work the next night. Ryan was kept busy making deliveries from the time he got to work until they closed. The thirty plus dollars he earned in tips would just about cover his insurance when added to his paycheck for the week.

"But it still doesn't leave me anything extra to take Laura to the prom," he complained to Matt. "If I could be sure of a couple more nights with tips like that, I'd be okay, but I'm afraid I'll have more nights like Friday."

The two boys lounged in the Maddoxes' basement

rec room. *Buckaroo Banzai* was in its umpteenth rerun on HBO and they talked between their favorite parts.

"Don't sweat it. She knows you're strapped for cash. Laura isn't like Therese; she doesn't expect you to spend a fortune on her every time you take her out."

"I don't want her to think I'm cheap."

"She won't. There's no law that says we have to rent a tux. A lot of the guys wear suits or sport coats. We can always wear a tux when we're seniors."

"Yeah, I guess we could. I still have all the other stuff to pay for."

Matt gave Ryan a friendly nudge. "Laura is the most open and honest girl I know. Talk it over with her. I don't think she'd mind if you didn't take her to the best restaurant in town. She might even suggest skipping the dinner."

"I don't *want* to skip it," said Ryan irritably. "I'll find the money somehow."

"Her folks really said it's okay for her to go?"

Ryan made a wry face. "Believe it or not, it was having Cheryl there that convinced them I was okay. Her mother thinks any guy who'd bring along his sister must be the right stuff. She doesn't know how close I came to strangling my dear little sister."

"I'm sure glad Sue and I are the youngest kids in the family. Of course, I still have her dad to deal with. He let me know he'll be waiting up for her whenever we go out."

Ryan grinned and tossed a pillow at his friend. "So how are you and Sue getting along? She still fluttering those eyelashes at you?"

"Not as much as she used to. I still turn to water

everytime she does.'' He sighed happily. ''Did you ever notice how good girls smell?''

''Laura always smells like a walk in the woods after a rain. Clean and fresh. She told me what kind of perfume it is but I never can remember the name.''

''Sue wears some kind of flowery stuff. Not exactly roses but it smells like it might have roses in it.''

''I don't like that heavy stuff some girls wear. Therese wore some one time that gave me a headache.''

''I know what you mean. When Sue puts her arms around me and lays her head on my shoulder and looks at me with those big brown eyes, it's all I can do to keep my hands off her.''

''Yeah, I have that same problem with Laura, but I know if I ever tried anything funny, it would be the end of the line. Still, I like being with her better than being with Therese.''

''Speaking of Therese, what do you think will happen to her now? Your boss wasn't really going to put her name on that letter she's sending around, was she?''

Ryan shrugged. ''I don't know. I'm not even sure she'll really send the letter. It could have been just a threat. As ticked off as she was the other night, I didn't want to ask questions.''

''Well, I don't think it's fair for Jeff to get all the blame. Therese probably put him up to it.''

''I'm sure she did. She heard me telling Mike Bergstrom that I'd gotten a job there. I still can't figure her, all the times she turned me down, yet she acts like Laura stole me away. It's stupid!''

''One thing for sure, the whole school will know about it Monday, whether there's any letter or not.

Bad news travels faster than the speed of light around Lockwood.''

"You're telling me." Though he'd never admit it, Ryan was worried he'd be branded a narc.

Jeff's father reacted in a way nobody expected. He put Jeff's car in storage until the end of the school year. Jeff was demoted to riding the bus or begging a ride from friends. Mr. Yarbrough must have made an impression because Jeff bluntly told his friends the whole thing was Therese's fault, not Ryan's.

Therese suddenly found herself as popular as an extra week of school. Word soon circulated that Therese had also been the one behind the ugly gossip about Ryan and Laura. The kids might have tolerated that, but robbing Ryan was the last straw.

"Therese gets dumber every day," marveled Craig at lunch on Monday. "First she smears Laura, then she circulates that so-called diary about your hot love affair, now she makes Jeff lose his wheels. There isn't a guy in this school who'll touch her."

"Not if it's going to cost him his car," said Jason.

Peter looked at Ryan. "Your boss really did blacklist them. My sister has a friend who works at Shakey's and she saw the letter. Can you imagine not being able to get a pizza delivered by *anybody?*"

"Seriously, guys," said Ryan, "what would you have done in my shoes—let them rip you off or report them?"

"Report them," said Craig promptly. "I work too hard for my dough to let somebody else take it. By the time the deductions come out of my check, that pizza would have cost me a whole night's pay."

Peter agreed. "Same here. When you work for slave wages, you don't throw it away. Not all of us have an old man who hands out money like Jeff's does.''

''What did Laura say about it?'' asked Jason curiously.

Ryan grinned. ''She said it was blackmail, not robbery. When I thought about them pulling that week after week, I reported them.''

''I make it a policy never to agree with Laura,'' said Craig, ''but this time she's right on. We have a lot of trouble with shoplifters at the record shop, especially kids trying to rip off tapes. If I saw somebody from school and didn't report it, I'd be canned.''

''Same with my job at the store,'' added Jason. ''I'm only a bag boy, like Matt, but you'd be surprised how often I see somebody trying to steal groceries.''

Ryan looked around the table and inwardly sighed with relief. His friends finally accepted Laura.

Chapter 9

"I guess being ripped off had its good side after all," said Ryan.

He and Laura sat on the grass in her backyard, planning a picnic for Sunday afternoon. The gang planned to meet at Melody Lake, a group event approved by Laura's parents.

Laura nudged him affectionately. "We've got only four weeks of school left, so maybe things will shake out over the summer. By the time school starts again, I'll be ready to sell my memoirs about our hot romance to the *National Enquirer*."

Ryan choked, giving her a sharp look. "Don't say that too loud. If your mother hears you, she'll veto the picnic. Or send Tim along to chaperone."

"He has a Scout camp-out and canoe trip this weekend." She grinned broadly, getting an equally broad grin from Ryan.

"That's the best news I've heard in days. All of us guys are bringing our baseball gear and Jason's bringing his Frisbee. Or we could rent a canoe and paddle around the lake."

"Yes to all of the above," said Laura, laughing. "Sue isn't much for sports but then she's never had any brothers. Matt can take her for a romantic ride in the canoe.''

Ryan stretched out on his stomach, plucking at blades of grass. It was a bright, sunny day with just enough breeze to keep them from feeling the heat. Nearby, a lilac bush bloomed in full glory, perfuming the surrounding area.

"I've been looking for another job for summer. There's a possibility I might get one at the plywood veneer place," said Ryan.

"I've heard they pay good money."

"Better than most jobs for high school kids. The hours are kind of crazy. They don't have air conditioning so the manager says they start work at five A.M. during July and August, when it's so hot, and quit at two."

"My gosh, you'd have to get up at four."

Ryan tilted his head toward her. "About then, and I never have been fond of getting up early."

Rolling over on his back, Ryan shaded his eyes with his arm. Laura stretched out beside him, propping her chin up on one elbow. With the other hand, she traced the letters on his T-shirt. He caught her hand and raised it to his lips.

"Watch it, Lover Boy," she teased. "Such raging passion might shock the neighbors."

"Please don't call me that," he said quietly.

Laura glanced at him in surprise. "Okay. I thought you liked it."

"I used to, when I was dumb enough to think it was a compliment. All those stories were more talk than truth anyway. Not just with Therese, with all the girls."

"That's what I've always thought, Ryan."

"It is?" Ryan jerked his arm away from his eyes to look into hers. "Honest?"

"Honest. Do you really believe I wouldn't have dropped you when the attacks started if I thought those stories were true? I've known Therese since we were in kindergarten and she's always been boy crazy. She *loves* being known as the sexiest girl in school."

"That's not exactly how I'd describe her," said Ryan dryly.

"Ryan, Sue and I aren't as naive or innocent as you and Matt seem to think. We've heard the way boys talk about Therese. We've heard the way *girls* talk about her. Even at the worst, none of the girls talked about me like that. They all knew, deep down, that Therese was full of hot air when she wrote that stuff about us."

"That's not the word I'd have chosen, but I agree with the sentiment."

Laura gazed at him steadily. "Sometimes I get the feeling you and Matt think Sue and I are plaster saints. We aren't. We want to be treated with respect but you don't have to treat us with kid gloves."

Ryan shifted his gaze to the rose bushes bordering the pool. He'd bet money she'd never dreamed about him the way he dreamed about her.

"Laura, I've had enough experience to know that you haven't had much, and it's not because I've gone around asking." He sat up, hooking his arms around his knees. "Look, the Lover Boy stuff was exaggerated, but there was some truth to it."

"I can accept that."

"Good." He kissed her fingers again. "You haven't dated much, have you?"

"No. Not many boys have enough self-confidence

to date a feminist. They prefer girls like Sue. She doesn't threaten them."

He chuckled. "Yeah, she probably doesn't threaten to punch them out or break their knees or scalp them."

Laura threw a handful of grass at him. "I gave you a fair chance to refuse."

"Like Benedick, I took you out of pity."

"That was one of his choicer lines. I don't remember what Beatrice said, but it wasn't that good."

"That's where he 'stopped her mouth' with a kiss."

"Right. I was so busy preparing to defend myself against your attack that I didn't pay much attention to the words."

"Have you ever dated Peter?" Ryan felt his stomach tense up at the question. Why was he so curious about the animosity Peter always expressed toward Laura?

"Which one? I know four boys named Peter."

"Peter McCabe."

"Oh, him. No. Why?" She regarded him quizzically.

"Just wondered. Seems to be a lot of tension between the two of you, and I thought maybe you'd gone out with him sometime and didn't get along."

It took a minute for her to answer, then she seemed uncomfortable answering his question. She focused her attention on the grass, avoiding his eyes completely. It made Ryan feel uneasy.

"You might say we had a difference of opinion in the past. I tend to get carried away when I care about something and he didn't like it. Ever since then he's made cracks about getting off my soapbox, stuff like that."

Ryan thought it over. He felt that there was something Laura didn't want him to know, but he decided

141

not to press. "Yeah, I didn't think you two had ever dated. Speaking of dates, the prom is definitely okay?"

"Yes, but there's another problem. I know you're a little short of money now, so I think I should help with the cost." She sat up to put her hand over his mouth before he could object. "Listen to what I have to say before you start yelling. Mom bought one of those coupon books the Jaycees were selling. You know the kind?"

"The kind that if you have a tune-up, you get a free oil change?"

"On that order. Anyway, one of the coupons is for five dollars off any purchase at the Shrinking Violet Flower Shoppe. You could get my corsage there."

"Yeah, I guess that would be okay," conceded Ryan after a moment's thought.

"Another coupon gives you one dinner free when you buy one, if you don't mind a family-type restaurant. Not a whole lot of atmosphere but good food. And it's good for up to four people, so we could ask Sue and Matt to go with us."

Ryan gazed at her steadily. "You know something, Laura, I think you're the nicest girl I've ever met. I'm only sorry it took me so long to find it out."

"Thank you." His compliment brought a sparkle to her eyes. "We can split the cost of the tickets and the pictures."

"I can pay for it, as long as you don't mind if I go in a suit instead of a tux."

"Personally, I've always thought a tux was a colossal waste of money. I don't mean to pry, but are you sure it won't leave you short on your insurance payment?"

"I can swing it. One of the neighbors hired me to

142

mow her lawn for the summer, so that gives me a little extra cash.''

"If anything comes up and you're going to be short—"

He cut her off with a kiss. "Don't worry. Thanks for your help. And I'll make it up to you, Laura, I promise."

"I don't gauge how much a boy likes me by how much money he spends on me. It's how he spends his *time* that counts."

Ryan grinned. "I don't have enough of that to spend on you, either. Your father keeps sending me home before midnight." He hesitated a moment, then asked, "Would you have gone out with me a second time if it hadn't been for the smear campaign? It's not just to prove a point?"

Laura gave him an incredulous look, then laughed. "You know, for a self-admitted genius, you ask some really stupid questions."

They had another sunny day for their picnic, with just a hint of a breeze. Laura waited for Ryan on the front porch step. As he pulled up, she ran to meet him, looking very pretty in a white ruffled peasant blouse and red cotton pants. Ryan was glad he'd worn his red-and-white jams.

"As beautiful as you are today, I'm not sure I should take you out in public," he said, slipping an arm around her waist. "Somebody might try to steal you away."

She squeezed his waist. "There you go, trying to get rid of me again. Even if you drowned me in the lake, I'd come back and haunt you."

"Speaking of the lake, do you think it's warm enough for swimming? It's supposed to go to eighty today, but that's a big lake and the ice hasn't been off that long.''

"I packed my suit anyway, just in case.''

"We'll have to swing back by my place then.''

Laura went to her room to get her beach bag, leaving Ryan to visit with her father. When she returned, Ryan picked up the ice chest from the kitchen table and followed her out to the car. He put it on the back seat and Laura tossed her bag beside it.

"I hope you don't mind onions in the potato salad,'' said Laura. "I thought about leaving them out but no onions is really blah.''

Ryan grinned, momentarily diverting his eyes from the road to his companion. "As long as we both eat it, it shouldn't make any difference. We're probably going to have ten times more food than we need anyway, with all of us bringing something.''

"Fine. By the way, I may have another job this summer. Mrs. Overacker has a friend who owns a needlecraft boutique and she's planning to offer lessons in cross-stitching, candlewicking, and needlepoint. Anyway, she needs a salesclerk to take care of the customers while she's teaching.''

"Hey, that's terrific. Will you get paid any more?''

"Only because I'm working more hours. It's still basic slavery when it comes to cold cash.''

"How well I know. Dad's on my case about saving half of each check for college and he *knows* what a hard time I had just trying to get my insurance paid. Sometimes I think he thinks prices are still the same as they were when he was a kid.''

"I know. My father asked me the other day what I thought my chances were for a scholarship. I told him somewhere between remote and nonexistent.''

"I think I might have a small chance with either

football or basketball scholarships, depending on what kind of a season we have next year. The only drawback is, I'll probably get offers from small private colleges and I'd like to go to the U of M. I'm not in their league.''

Laura waited in the car while Ryan ran inside to get his swimsuit and a towel. Cheryl waved from the side lawn. Ryan thrust his gym bag at Laura and speedily reversed the car out of the driveway, then took off down the street. Laura grabbed the side of her seat, alarmed.

"What's the rush?" she demanded.

"Mom was on the phone, talking to Grandma, and I heard her ask them to come over. I didn't want Mom getting any bright ideas about having us hang around so you could meet them. Not that I think they wouldn't like you,'' he hastily amended.

"I know what you mean,'' said Laura, laughing. "Narrow escape.''

Laura twisted around in her seat to put his gym bag in back. It landed on hers, then slid to the floor with a thud, out of her reach.

"Don't worry about it,'' said Ryan. "It's okay there.''

"What do you want to take in college that you couldn't get at a small one?''

"It might sound silly, but someday I'd like to build rockets for real. I've done a lot of reading about uni-directional drive and I think we'll have to master it before interplanetary travel is practical.''

Laura gazed at him in wide-eyed wonder. "What is uni . . . whatever you said?''

"How simple do you want the explanation?''

"Simple enough for somebody who consistently

recognizes the page numbers in the trig book and not much else.''

Ryan laughed. ''That's getting pretty basic. In simple terms, it's the force that makes the planets revolve in their orbits. You should be able to use that same kind of force to send a rocket into space and have it return to its point of origin, just as if it were in orbit.''

''Oh. If you ever figure it out, get a patent on it. It ought to be worth a dollar or two from the Pentagon.''

When they reached the end of Third, Ryan slowly merged into the traffic heading for Melody Lake. From the looks of things, half the population had just emerged from hibernation to enjoy the warm weather.

''So what do you want to do, be the first woman President?''

''By the time I'm old enough, we'll probably already have one, so you can just wipe that chauvinistic grin off your face,'' said Laura, pretending to be mad. ''Don't forget Geraldine Ferraro. I'd like to go into counseling, maybe work with battered wives or abused children. They need to know how to stand up for their rights.''

''You're the one to tell them,'' said Ryan, a trifle too emphatically.

''I'm serious! You wouldn't believe the number of women who let their husbands beat them time after time and refuse to file charges. If my husband ever laid a hand on me, I'd brain him with the largest, heaviest object I could lift!''

''*That* I believe,'' said Ryan. ''Take a look at that parking lot! The whole county must be here today.''

Ryan found a Bug-sized spot fairly close to the picnic area. He carried the cooler while Laura carried the beach bags and blanket. They selected a grassy area under the large sycamore they'd set as a meeting place and spread the blanket.

"Looks like we're ahead of the rest of the gang. Before we have those onions . . ." Ryan pulled her close for a kiss. "How's that for chauvinistic behavior?"

"I don't believe in making snap judgments. We'll have to repeat the experiment several times."

He kissed her again. "Kissing you is more fun since you gave up wearing that mask."

"I was so scared somebody might guess I liked you when we had to read that story. That's why I wanted you to get out of it."

Ryan stared at her in disbelief. "That's what Matt said!"

"He knew?" Laura looked ready to cry.

"He guessed. And he guessed I liked you. Maybe we were more like Beatrice and Benedick than we thought."

"Do you think anybody else guessed?"

Ryan considered it. "Maybe Mrs. Kingsley. I don't remember her exact words but she thought we were perfect for the parts. She wasn't about to let me get out of it, even when Matt offered to trade."

"That explains that peculiar remark she made after I asked you to come over to my house. When I came into class the next time, she smiled and said, 'I make a pretty good Prince, don't I?' I couldn't figure out what she was talking about."

A puzzled frown furrowed Ryan's brow. "Prince?"

"The Prince was the one who thought up the plot to make Beatrice and Benedick fall in love."

They heard a shout and turned to see Jason, Tanya, Craig, and Peter coming toward them. Craig was playing the field at the moment and Peter's girlfriend,

Nikki, was out of town for the weekend. They added their stuff to the pile by the tree and spread more blankets.

"Matt will be along as soon as he finds a parking place," said Craig. "Which might be midnight."

It was another ten minutes before Matt and Sue joined the group. Matt looked flushed, as if trying hard to control his temper. Even Sue looked a little flustered.

Ryan slapped him on the back. "Sorry I didn't think to offer you a ride."

"No problem. I should have had brains enough to ask for Mom's Honda instead of bringing my battleship. I saw *three* places I could have gotten into with a smaller car."

"We're all here," said Peter, "so let's forget the nightmare we had parking or may have later if everybody decides to leave at once. What do we do first?"

They all stood there, looking at each other, no one wanting to take the lead. A trip to the lake's edge proved the water still too cold for anyone but a polar bear. The canoes were all gone, but they put their names down for a couple of rowboats between two and three.

"We can do that after we eat, give lunch time to settle," said Ryan.

Laura nodded. "It's just after noon now. We can toss around the Frisbee for a while, then eat."

Jason dazzled them all with his expertise. He'd won a city-wide contest last summer, sponsored by a local sporting goods store. As winner, he'd received a $100 gift certificate to the store, which he'd spent on skiing equipment, then broken his ankle the second time out. Since then, he'd decided Frisbee was his game.

Ryan was right about a surplus of food. Even five hollow-legged teenaged boys couldn't put it all away. Ryan lay back on the blanket, folded his hands loosely across his full stomach and closed his eyes.

"Does that funereal pose mean you expect to die of food poisoning at any minute?" teased Laura.

"It means I couldn't possibly marry you. I'd weigh a ton in a week."

"No, you wouldn't," said Laura, laughing. "I expect my husband to take turns with the cooking and cleaning."

He opened one eye. "After three days of eating my cooking, you'd give up those liberated ideas. Maybe after one meal."

"He's right," said Matt, turning to Peter. "Remember when we were in Scouts and Ryan was supposed to cook spaghetti for one of our camp-outs?"

"Yeah. He put the lid on and left it. You should have seen it—one solid lump. Gross."

Tanya gave him a curious look. "Did you eat it?"

"Are you kidding? We opened a couple cans of beans instead." Peter grinned at the memory. "We put the spaghetti blob in Buster's sleeping bag. Remember Buster Cunningham? The fat kid with all the zits?"

Everybody had a favorite Buster story to share. When they'd finished, they put the leftover food away and took turns in the boats. That left them ready for a game of baseball. Matt looked at the mob now on all sides of them.

"We can't play here," he said. "We'll have to go to the open area on the other side of the parking lot, and we'd better take our stuff with us."

Everybody grabbed an armload and headed toward the parking lot, detouring to put away stuff they no longer needed. They passed the horseshoe pits, where a group of senior citizens were having a match, then another group playing volleyball. By the time they found a large enough free space, they were almost to the border between the park and the private summer cottages.

After marking out a rough diamond, they split up into teams. Tanya, who was pitcher for the girls' softball team, was a remarkably good player and Laura managed to hold her own. Only Sue consistently struck out, no matter how patiently Matt tried to coach her. She would have preferred being a spectator, but that would have left one team short a person.

They were in the top of the seventh inning, Ryan's team leading five to four, when Peter came up to bat. Ryan was on the pitcher's mound, Matt catching, Laura covering first base, and Sue stationed between second and third. Ryan pitched a perfect ball. Peter connected with a powerful drive that sent the ball right through the window of the nearest cottage. Everyone froze.

Peter swore once, then looked directly at Laura. They gazed into each other's eyes for a long moment. There was something in that gaze that excluded everyone else, and Ryan couldn't begin to read what it meant. "I guess I'd better go talk to the people," Peter finally said, dropping his bat.

The moment she heard his words, Laura gave him a dazzling smile that sent a stab of jealousy through Ryan. What was between those two? Laura had only smiled at him a few times like that and he definitely didn't like seeing her smile the same way at Peter.

The cottage owner was an elderly woman with

bright hennaed hair. She returned the ball, refusing Peter's offer to pay for the window.

"You've done me a big favor, young man," she said, smiling smugly. "I've been trying to get my husband to replace that solid window with a louvered window for years, and he's such an old skinflint he wouldn't do it. I've been tempted to throw a rock through it myself. Now I'll finally have a window I can open."

That put an end to their game and a damper on the picnic. They finished off the food, then went their separate ways.

On the drive home, Ryan started to ask Laura several times about the significance of that look and smile. Somehow, he couldn't get the words out. He was probably making a mountain out of a molehill, and he didn't want her to think he was the jealous type, not after that incident with Therese.

It wasn't until he'd dropped Laura off and was on the way home that the obvious solution hit him.

"I can ask Peter."

Chapter 10

Ryan planned to ask Peter—*casually*—about the incident at lunch the next day. Peter didn't show up at lunch. Craig, who was in the same third-hour English class, said Peter had left at ten-forty-five for a dental appointment and would probably stop at McDonald's for lunch.

"I would if I were him," said Matt. "This pita pocket is so dry, it makes their barf on a bun look good."

Jason gave him a smug grin. "I told you, you should have gotten the chili and cornbread. Chili and lasagna are two things this cafeteria does good."

"Peter sure lucked out with that broken window," said Craig.

That led to a general discussion of how bad it could have been and how none of them had ever been that lucky. Though Ryan listened carefully, not one of them mentioned the silent exchange between Laura and Peter. Maybe it was just his imagination.

Ryan thought the subject was closed until Cheryl sauntered into his room just before supper. He was sitting at his desk, working out what he hoped would be a winning entry in a model rocket design contest.

The company offered a prize of $100 for the best entry.

"Did you see the flowers Peter gave Laura?" she asked, perching on his bed.

Ryan instantly went on the alert. "What flowers?"

"One of those mixed bouquets of carnations, daisies, you know, like you get at the supermarket. He dropped them off after school. I saw them when I was over there helping Tim get their pool ready for summer. Tim said Laura laughed when she read the card, but I didn't see anything funny about it."

"What did it say?" He realized he sounded too anxious, but at the moment, he didn't feel confident enough to play it cool. It was bad enough that Peter gave her flowers; he didn't have to deliver them himself!

Cheryl screwed up her face, as if trying to remember. "Something about four years late to apologize. Tim didn't know what it meant, and I didn't think it would be polite to ask Laura."

"No, it wouldn't." He turned back to his design, dismissing Cheryl. Unfortunately, he couldn't dismiss his growing jealousy.

After supper, a grimly determined Ryan drove to the McCabe house. Mrs. McCabe was weeding her flower border and told Ryan that Peter was in back. Walking around the two-story colonial, he found Peter practicing his golf swing. Peter watched his approach, warily defensive. Ryan didn't waste any breath on preliminaries.

"Why are you giving flowers to *my* girl?"

"It's a long, dull story and has nothing to do with you or trying to horn in on your girl. I figured I owed her an apology for all the years I've been bitching about her." He saw Ryan's scowl deepen. "Hey, they were only four bucks at the supermarket and I gave them to her myself; it's not like I ordered fancy roses and had a florist deliver them.''

"Yeah. Well, I've got lots of time and I don't mind long, dull stories," said Ryan flatly. He gave Peter an intense scrutiny, as if trying to see inside his head. "What's between you and Laura?" he asked quietly. "You've always been down on her more than the other guys."

Peter exhaled loudly and averted his eyes. "Okay. I guess you're not going to let me off easy. When we were in junior high, I shot rubber bands at the kids in front of me. One even hit the teacher. She never caught me because I sat in the back corner and Laura was the only one who ever saw me. One day, Mrs. Franke said she'd keep the whole class after school for three days if anybody shot more rubber bands. Well, I didn't believe her, so I kept it up."

"And she kept you all after school."

"Right. I didn't think she'd really make us stay the whole three days but she did. I kept waiting for Laura to tell on me. She expected me to confess. That last day, she came over here on her bike, mad enough to take me apart. She said if I ever did anything like that again, she'd stand up in class and hit me over the head with her book."

Ryan's eyes narrowed. "That's it?" He didn't believe it. "Why would you stay mad all these years because she threatened to hit you with a book?"

Peter turned his back and took a vicious swing at the air with his iron. Ryan waited for an answer, refusing to leave until he got one. Reluctantly, Peter faced him, pain clearly visible in his eyes.

"There's a little more to it than that," he said slowly. He paused for a long moment. "We go to the

154

same church. When we were in the eighth grade, we had a Youth Fellowship party at Christmas. Laura wore a blue velvet dress, just the color of her eyes.'' He looked at Ryan. "Have you ever noticed what pretty eyes she has?''

"Quite a few times,'' said Ryan dryly. The fact that Peter had noticed them didn't do anything for his temper.

"She was so happy and excited at that party . . . I noticed her eyes for the first time. The way they were sparkling made her look beautiful.'' He stopped again.

Ryan could well imagine how she looked. He felt a mixture of jealousy and compassion for his friend, knowing full well the effect of Laura's eyes.

"Some of us guys hid mistletoe in the decorations over the door between the hall and the big community room. You couldn't really see it unless you knew it was there. I waited for my chance and kissed Laura when she went out to get a drink of water. On the cheek,'' he hastily added, seeing Ryan's face darken.

"She told me you never dated.'' Jealousy now dominated compassion.

"We didn't. She blushed and giggled, then she ran back with the other girls. When we had refreshments, she let me sit beside her. The only time I saw her was at church, until we moved into this house during spring vacation and I transferred to the same school. I thought she might like me when we were together more often.''

"Did she?''

Peter made a couple more swings. "I think she was starting to, until the rubber band business. I felt bad about getting the whole class in trouble, then I was afraid the guys might beat me up if I admitted it.''

''Did they know it was you?''

''Some of them asked if it was me but Laura was the only one who knew for sure. When she didn't report me, I figured it was because she liked me.''

Ryan shoved his hands in his pockets, staring at his feet. Laura must have liked Peter a lot to keep quiet about it. Or maybe it was like the lipstick in the john, she preferred to handle it herself.

''When she came over, she said she expected me to be man enough to accept responsibility instead of letting the whole class suffer. You know Laura and her principles. She expects everybody else to have the same principles and the kind of guts she has.''

Ryan knew by the expression on Peter's face how much that had hurt. Peter focused his eyes on a distant tree. His voice grew so soft that Ryan had to strain to hear him.

''It hurts when a girl stops liking you. It goes deeper when she stops respecting you.'' He gave his head a quick shake, then continued, louder. ''When I broke that damned window yesterday, the whole rubber band business flashed through my mind again. I knew Laura expected me to do the right thing.''

''What's that got to do with the flowers?''

''I was at the store getting some stuff for my mother and they were in a big plastic pail by the check-out lane. I didn't think about how it might look to you; I just got them. It made me feel better, you know? For the first time in four years, I can actually look that girl in the eyes without feeling guilty.''

Ryan didn't mention the flowers to Laura. She

brought it up the next day on the way home from school, telling pretty much the same story.

"And if you think you're the only one who's felt any jealousy, you're crazy," she finished. "When I saw Therese kiss you that day, for about ten seconds, I felt like murdering both of you."

"I didn't say I was jealous."

"You didn't have to. It wasn't until I was getting ready for bed Sunday night that I finally figured out what was eating you after that game. You barely spoke to me on the way home. You just kept saying you were tired."

He broke into a grin. "Okay, I was jealous. And you were so evasive when I asked you about Peter, I figured something had to have gone on between you."

"I didn't want to tell tales on Peter. I know he's one of your best friends. But you don't have anything to worry about—I'm glad Peter and I can be friends now, but that's all I want to be with him."

When Laura walked into the Nettleton living room Saturday night, Ryan knew she'd be the prettiest girl at the prom. Her gown was some kind of soft filmy material in pale blue with puffed sleeves and lace ruffles. Rhinestones sparkled at her ears and throat.

"Mom let me borrow them for the occasion," she told him. "If I lose them, I'll be shot at dawn. She got this set as part of her official prizes when she was Strawberry Festival Queen. These rhinestones are the closest thing we've got to family jewels."

A red carnation decorated the lapel of Ryan's navy suit. Laura gave it to him when he presented her corsage of red roses. Pinning the flowers on each other proved to be harder than it looked. Ryan was afraid her parents might think he was trying to get

157

fresh when he fumbled with the pin, trying to get it through the corsage and dress simultaneously. Laura's mother finally came to his rescue.

"Now we're color coordinated," Laura said, then added, "Actually I'm branding you to let other girls know they'd better keep their hands off."

Laura's mom made them wait long enough for her to take pictures in front of the fireplace, then walked out to the car where Matt and Sue waited so she could see Sue's dress. Since Matt had the bigger car, he drove, first to the restaurant for dinner, then to the hotel where the prom was being held.

Gold and brown, the school colors of Lockwood High, decorated the Holiday Inn ballroom. Each table held two brown candles on either side of a yellow rose. A mirrored ball turned slowly overhead. The band played from a small platform at one end of the room with the refreshment table to the left of it. An adult chaperone served punch.

"Is that really Mrs. Crawley?" asked Ryan, nodding toward the tall woman near the door.

Laura craned her neck, trying to see over the crowd. "It looks vaguely like her. She had her hair done, just like the rest of us girls. And that black gown makes her look thinner."

Matt joined them in peering at their principal. "Jeez, I hope we guys aren't expected to dance with her."

"Leave that to the chaperones," said Ryan. "They aren't here to enjoy themselves."

They shared a table with Peter and Nikki. Neither Craig nor Jason had come. Ryan didn't know Nikki, a tenth grade girl from Peter's photography class. She looked younger than Cheryl and kept pulling up the top of her teal strapless dress. Sue had no need to pull up the top of her strapless pink gown.

"There isn't a chance it'll fall down," Matt whispered to Ryan when the girls were busy talking.

Ryan winked. "I don't think anybody would ever mistake her for a boy. Dolly Parton, maybe."

Looking around, Ryan noticed that about forty percent of the boys were in suits rather than tuxedoes or dinner jackets. Not all the girls wore long dresses either; several were in cocktail-length dresses and a few in silky pants and blouses.

Mrs. Crawley circulated through the ballroom frequently, making sure there weren't any flasks adding zip to the punch or soft drinks. Three years ago, she'd caught a boy slipping lab alcohol into the punch bowl. The boy, a senior, was suspended for two weeks and not allowed to march at graduation. Nobody had tried anything like that since. Some of the kids thought it would be cool to put one over on Old Hatchet Face, but none of them wanted to risk parental wrath if caught.

After the band took their second break, Matt suggested they trade partners for one dance. Ryan agreed, perfectly willing to dance with Sue. She did smell like roses. They slowly circled the ballroom, Sue easily following him. He didn't hold her as close as he held Laura, but then Matt was keeping Laura at a respectable distance, too.

"I'm glad you and Laura finally got together. She's liked you for a long time."

Ryan looked down at Sue, a little surprised. "Did she tell you that?"

"Mm-hmm, but I knew it anyway. She always gets gets so tense when a new semester starts because she's afraid you might not be in any of her classes.

She could never ask what your schedule was because she didn't want anybody to guess she cared if you were there or not.''

''Yeah?''

''She always told me it would be a real relief not to have to endure you, but anytime you were absent, she worried about it. It really upset her when the kids started calling you Lover Boy. She said she'd always thought you were a nice boy, not the kind to get mixed up with somebody like Therese Deauville.''

Ryan was so intent on this unexpected fountain of information that he didn't notice Matt and Peter trade partners on the other side of the ballroom. When he swung Sue around in that direction and saw Laura in Peter's arms, he momentarily froze. Peter didn't have to hold her that close! Ryan headed toward them as fast as he could at this slow tempo. Before he reached his objective, the ballroom lights flickered, then went out.

''Everyone stand still,'' boomed the voice of the band leader. ''We'll get the lights back on in a minute. It's just a short in the fuse from all our instruments. We had a few problems with it last week. We don't want you crashing into each other; somebody might get hurt.''

Ryan swore under his breath, involuntarily tightening his hold on Sue. Peter was the last person on earth he wanted Laura to be with in the dark, now that they were on friendly terms! If Peter tried anything . . .

Someone near them flicked on a lighter. A few other lights popped up around the room. Ryan wished he had one.

''Careful with those lighters, people,'' said the band leader. ''We don't want anyone burned.''

Ryan dropped the hand he had on Sue's shoulder-blade, still holding her hand. "Aren't they ever going to get these lights fixed?" he grumbled.

"I hope so. You'd think they'd know how to fix it in a hurry if it's happened before."

Just as Ryan was ready to follow a lighter moving toward the sidelines, the lights came back on. He quickly looked for Laura and Peter. They weren't where he'd last seen them.

"Let's go sit down," said Sue. "The others will probably come back to the table."

Ryan let her take the lead while he continued to scan the room. He'd just held Sue's chair for her to sit down when Laura and Peter came up behind him.

"I hope we don't have any more surprises like that. What do you think caused it?" asked Laura. She looked up at Ryan, who was staring at Peter's white dinner jacket. Laura followed his gaze. Her pink lipstick was smeared on one lapel. "Oh, Peter, I'm sorry!"

Peter glanced down at it. "Must have happened when that clown bumped into us. How's your foot?"

"I won't have to walk with a limp for more than five or six weeks. He felt like he weighed a ton. I hope that lipstick comes out."

"I'll ask my mother if she has something to take it out. If not, the people at the tux shop probably have."

Matt and Nikki arrived on the scene and the group immediately started exchanging stories of "where were you when the lights went out." Ryan sat there, not saying a word, his face grim. Laura eventually noticed it and pulled his head down to whisper in his ear.

"Stop looking like such a thundercloud. It's not

Peter's fault the lights went out and he didn't try anything funny. Somebody crashed into us and pushed me against him." Ryan continued to glower. Laura quickly kissed his ear. "If I'd been dancing with you then, the lipstick wouldn't be on your jacket!"

He slowly relaxed, then grinned at her. "I don't handle jealousy very well, do I? I'm not taking any more chances. You're dancing with me for the rest of the night."

When he kissed her good night, he held her tightly, half afraid to let her go. "I love you," he whispered. "Crazy, isn't it? A month ago, you were my favorite enemy."

He was rewarded with a kiss that set him reeling. Skyrockets seemed to be going off inside his head and his blood pressure reached a new high.

"I love you, too, Ryan. I love you so much."

He went home happier than he'd ever been in his life.

A heatwave surged through the state the end of May making the Nettleton pool a very popular place, since it was one of the few private pools in their section of town. Ryan and Cheryl spent all their free time there. Matt and Sue were also invited to share the pool frequently.

By a combination of unexpected events, Laura and Ryan found themselves alone in the pool one Saturday afternoon. Her parents were out golfing. Cheryl was at a birthday party, and Tim decided to go watch baseball on a neighbor's closed circuit TV. Laura had the day off due to another weekend trip by her boss and Ryan didn't need a second invitation to cool off before going to work.

Ryan wore a red swimsuit that gave the odd illusion that his slight sunburn was a reflection from his trunks. Laura sat on the edge of the pool, dangling her feet and watching him try to swim the length of the pool underwater. He made it on the third try.

"Super Lobster wins again," she cheered.

He pulled himself out beside her. "Lobster is right. It takes half the summer for me to get a tan and Matt steps out the door for five minutes and has one. Disgusting."

"True. Sue's the same way. It's even more disgusting that she looks so great in a bikini."

Ryan glanced down at the blue-and-white Hawaiian print Laura wore. "There's nothing wrong with the way you look, honey." He winked. "Just as long as I have exclusive rights."

Laura laughed. "You have so much competition."

"I would have if more guys saw you in that bikini."

"Flattery will get you everywhere," crooned Laura, stretching up to kiss him.

The touch of her sun-warmed skin jolted through Ryan like a lightning bolt. He pulled her against him for a longer kiss which led to one still longer. His heart raced and blood pounded in his ears. Slowly, he bent her backward onto the tiles, his kisses increasing in intensity. It took a moment for it to seep into his consciousness that Laura was trying to push him away.

"Oh, Ryan, please stop!"

One look at her frightened eyes jerked him back to reality. He plunged back into the pool, racing to the other end. When he saw Laura run into the house, he quickly dashed to the family room for his clothes, then to his car. He couldn't face Laura. If she said anything, what would her family think, after they'd finally learned to trust Lover Boy?

He was grateful to find his own house empty when he got home. After changing, he returned to the car and drove aimlessly around town until it was time for work. No way did he want to be home if Laura came over. How would he ever face her at school?

Mrs. Enzio noticed his distraction, the fact that it seemed to get worse as the evening went on and guessed that it had something to do with Laura.

"What did you and your girl fight about?" she asked Ryan as they were closing up for the night.

Ryan flushed, too embarrassed to tell her. She gave him a jaundiced look and nodded her head.

"Right. Things got a little out of hand and she slapped you and told you to get lost."

"That wasn't it at all," denied Ryan quickly. "Not exactly." He didn't want to tell this woman he hardly knew something so personal.

Mrs. Enzio waited for him to expand on his answer. When she concluded he wouldn't, she again took the lead.

"Okay, that wasn't exactly the way it was. Unless she made a grab for you—and from the way you've talked about her, I don't think she would—you must be the one feeling guilty. How am I doing?"

Ryan grudgingly nodded.

"Uh-huh. You're too embarrassed to go back and apologize. Your pride is more important than your girl."

"It isn't my pride. It's just that . . ." Ryan stopped, thoroughly miserable. "Laura's a nice girl. I don't want to do anything to hurt her."

"You've hurt her by leaving her." Ryan refused to respond to that. "Let me give you some advice from a woman who's been married four times. That girl can stop you anytime she wants to, so stop worrying about it. Women have a very well-developed instinct for self-preservation. One more thing, it was Eve who gave Adam the apple, so don't think you men have a corner on carnal lust.''

Sunday afternoon Ryan found himself approaching the Nettleton door once again with a cactus in hand. This one had a tiny pink ribbon pinned to the top. He wore his navy pants and blue-and-white-striped shirt, as if they were a talisman. He felt more nervous than he had the first time. If he blew it this time . . .

The surprised joy in Laura's eyes when she answered the door dissolved his fears. They just stood there for a moment, smiling at each other. All the speeches he'd rehearsed vanished from Ryan's mind.

"I thought it was about time Benedick met Beatrice," said Ryan, holding out the plant. "He's led the peaceful life of a bachelor long enough."

"He has been looking rather lonely lately. Let's introduce them."

Not exactly what he expected her to say, but better than having the door slammed in his face. His opening hadn't been too brilliant either. If his stomach would just stop churning. Had she said anything to her family about yesterday? Mrs. Enzio was the only one who'd pried anything out of him.

"Where is everybody?" asked Ryan nervously. He wasn't ready to be alone with Laura again so soon.

"Daddy's working on the computer in the basement, Mom is working on her tan by the pool, and Tim is hiding somewhere because he's supposed to mow the lawn and doesn't want to," said Laura, grinning.

"Sounds familiar." Knowing they were around dispelled some of Ryan's tension.

Laura asked Ryan to wait in the kitchen while she took the new cactus to her room. "Do you think we should leave them unchaperoned?" kidded Ryan, when Laura returned to the kitchen. He could have kicked himself. That was a stupid thing to say, considering.

"Don't worry, Beatrice isn't the kind of cactus to let a sexy succulent sweet-talk her."

If Laura could make light of it, so could he. "I don't know—I picked out Benedick in the first place because of the distinct twinkle in his eye."

"He's been lonely with no one to talk to," said Laura, a slight catch in her voice. "He needed someone who speaks his language. Want a Coke?"

"No." Ryan embraced her, holding her head against his shoulder. "Laura, I'm so sorry!"

He felt a sudden dampness on his shirt. Laura wrapped her arms around his waist, holding him tightly. "I was scared you wouldn't come back. I didn't mean to act like such a baby, running away, then you were gone . . . I know you're used to more-experienced girls."

Ryan kissed her tear-streaked cheek, then added a playful kiss to the tip of her nose. "I don't want those girls, I want *you*. I shouldn't have gotten carried away. It was like all my worst nightmares about those Lover Boy stories come true."

Laura wiped her tears, then sighed heavily. "Ryan, forget that Lover Boy crap. You were never really like that. I think the only reason Therese started it was because it made her sound like such hot stuff, getting you all turned on. Then she couldn't stand the idea of losing you to me, even when she didn't want you herself."

Ryan laughed. "You sure know how to do great things to a guy's ego."

"Ego? And here I thought I was affecting your libido. You sure affected mine," she replied, a little shyly.

"You're right. You affected my libido and I overreacted to the effect. No more kissing in bikinis. You're too irresistible."

"So are you." Laura smiled, leaning back in his arms to look up at him. "You're the sexiest lobster I've ever known."

"I don't know about you, Miss Nettleton. You may have to turn in your liberated ideas if you start thinking a parboiled lobster is sexy."

"Wrong. It's the sworn duty of every true feminist to convert a male chauvinist, even if it takes a lifetime. And it's not fair to run away from the battle."

"I won't again," he murmured. "I guess I did get too hung up on that Lover Boy tag. None of it was real. What I have with you is. I don't want to lose that."

"You won't. At least you won't if you abandon your evil ways and admit that woman really is the superior sex."

Ryan slowly backed up, putting the table between them. "Yeah, I admit women have always been superior in one aspect—getting in the last word. Like Benedick said when he kissed Beatrice, 'I will stop your mouth.' It's the only thing that ever works."

"Ryan Archer—" Laura stalked around the table after him, her grin broadening as Ryan backed himself into a corner.

"Really determined women wear hockey helmets with full face masks to get in the last word, but we won't drag that up—"

Laura stopped his mouth with a kiss.

LEILA DAVIS has been a high school substitute teacher for twenty-one years, drawing on her experiences for many of her stories about teenagers. She won the Romance Writers of America Golden Heart for best unpublished young adult novel in 1987, and LOVER BOY won the Northern Lights Writers' Contest later that year. Mrs. Davis has had articles and short stories published in magazines in the United States, Canada, England, Scotland, and Norway.

Says Mrs. Davis, "LOVER BOY developed from an incident at school. A boy was surprised and embarrassed to discover that a bad reputation can be as much of a problem for a boy as a girl."

The Davises have four children, two grandchildren, and reside in Kalamazoo, Michigan.

ATTENTION TEENAGE WRITERS!

You can win a $2,500 book contract and have your novel published as the winner of the 1989 Avon Flare Young Adult Novel Competition!

Here are the submission requirements:

We will accept completed manuscripts from authors between the ages of thirteen and eighteen from January 1, 1989 through August 31, 1989 at the following address:

The Editors, Avon Flare Novel Competition
Avon Books, Room 818, 105 Madison Avenue
New York, New York 10016

Each manuscript should be approximately 125 to 200 pages, or about 30,000 to 50,000 words (based on 250 words per page).

All manuscripts must be typed, double-spaced, on a single side of the page only.

Along with your manuscript, please enclose a letter that includes a short description of your novel, your name, address, telephone number, and your age.

You are eligible to submit a manuscript if you will be no younger than thirteen and no older than eighteen years of age as of December 31, 1988. Enclose a self-addressed, stamped envelope for the return of your manuscript, and a self-addressed stamped postcard so that we can let you know we have received your submission.

PLEASE BE SURE TO RETAIN A COPY OF YOUR MANUSCRIPT. WE CANNOT BE RESPONSIBLE FOR MANUSCRIPTS.

The Prize: If you win this competition your novel will be published by Avon Flare for an advance of $2,500.00 against royalties. A parent or guardian's signature (consent) will be required on your publishing contract.

We reserve the right to use the winning author's name and photograph for advertising, promotion, and publicity.

If you wish to be notified of the winner, please enclose a self-addressed, stamped postcard for this purpose. Notification will also be made to major media.

Waiting Time: We will try to review your manuscript within three months. However, it is possible that we will hold your manuscript for as long as a year, or until the winner is announced.

VOID WHERE PROHIBITED BY LAW.